This woman reminded him of the one he always remembered, the one who wouldn't let him go....

Reid grabbed Dani's arm, turned her toward him. Her smile was gone, and he wasn't sure. The face was Dani's—but the desire was the same. He closed his eyes, not wanting to see any more.

His lips touched hers and he was taken back to that night. He tasted her. Same taste. Was he losing his mind? His mouth turned hard and searching as he sank into a sensation that promised chaos and contentment and a sense of coming home—a home Reid had known only once before.

He pulled back even as his hands still clutched her shoulders. "I'm sorry. It won't happen again."

She tilted her head slowly up and looked at him. She, too, knew he was lying.

Dear Reader,

Every month Harlequin American Romance brings you four powerful men, and four admirable women who know what they want—and go all out to get it. Check out this month's sparkling selection of love stories, which you won't be able to resist.

First, our AMERICAN BABY promotion continues with Kara Lennox's *Baby by the Book*. In this heartwarming story, a sexy bachelor comes to the rescue when a pretty single mother goes into labor. The more time he spends with mother and child, the more he finds himself wanting the role of dad.…

Also available this month is *Between Honor and Duty* by Charlotte Maclay, the latest installment in her MEN OF STATION SIX series. Will a firefighter's determination to care for his friend's widow and adorable brood spark a vow to love, honor and cherish? Next, JUST FOR KIDS, Mary Anne Wilson's miniseries continues with an office romance between *The C.E.O. & the Secret Heiress*. And in *Born of the Bluegrass* by Darlene Scalera, a woman is reunited with the man she never stopped loving—the father of her secret child.

Enjoy this month's offerings, and be sure to return each and every month to Harlequin American Romance!

Wishing you happy reading,

Melissa Jeglinski
Associate Senior Editor
Harlequin American Romance

BORN OF THE
BLUEGRASS

Darlene Scalera

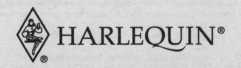

HARLEQUIN®

TORONTO • NEW YORK • LONDON
AMSTERDAM • PARIS • SYDNEY • HAMBURG
STOCKHOLM • ATHENS • TOKYO • MILAN • MADRID
PRAGUE • WARSAW • BUDAPEST • AUCKLAND

With gratitude to the women of the Winner's Circle, The Saratoga Romance Writers of America.

ISBN 0-373-16896-9

BORN OF THE BLUEGRASS

ABOUT THE AUTHOR

Darlene Scalera is a native New Yorker who graduated magna cum laude from Syracuse University with a degree in public communications. She worked in a variety of fields, including telecommunications and public relations, before devoting herself full-time to romance fiction writing. She was instrumental in forming the Saratoga, New York, chapter of Romance Writers of America and is a frequent speaker on romance writing at local schools, libraries, writing groups and women's organizations. She currently lives happily-ever-after in upstate New York with her husband, Jim, and their two children, J.J. and Ariana. You can write to Darlene at P.O. Box 217, Niverville, NY 12130.

Books by Darlene Scalera

HARLEQUIN AMERICAN ROMANCE

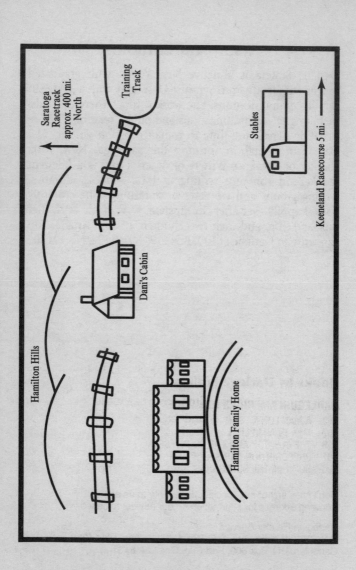

Prologue

Hamilton Hills Farm
Lexington, Kentucky

Reid woke. His hand reached, sliding across the sheet with the same care used to touch a Thoroughbred's million-dollar foreleg. The woman was gone. Where she had lain was still warm.

The night might have been a dream—the sky neither light nor dark, the evening song rising, too many people swaying beneath a white canopy. A heat. The scent of need. He had turned to greet yet another guest when he'd seen her. No sound had come from his parted lips. How long he had stared he didn't know. There was only the raging red of her hair, a jewel green dress, slim hips, elegant legs. An unknown wildness. The dream begun.

He gathered the sheet into his fist. It was here now. It'd been there then. From the first. Fire.

The woman had stared back, her hand rising to the bared skin above her breasts. Breasts that promised the taste of life. Her fingers had followed the long edge of her collarbone, lifted to the tender flesh where her jaw and neck met. There they'd rested as if reassuring him she was flesh and blood. Small swallows had rippled her throat as he'd moved toward her. He had put his hand on hers, felt the press of warmth, the flash of need. Fire.

Her name was Danielle DeVries, a debutante up from the Carolinas. She was here for the horses. Everyone was here for the horses. Her knees had swayed at the first touch of his lips to hers.

He was known for his ease with Thoroughbred horses and beautiful women. Many would say this was only one more night of many nights providing pleasure and passion. He would have agreed if he'd also been a curious observer or merely a clever participant. He hadn't. There'd been no room for wiles. He'd taken her in his arms and was no longer the master of his own fate. He'd been shaken, stunned, and, even now, craving more.

He sat up, fully awake, although his sleep had been little and his drinks had been many. He was content, restless, sated, wanting. Here was the magic they talked about. Who would have thought—a tip of the head, a curve of the neck, a meeting without warning? He would never underestimate life again.

He gathered his clothes, dressed, left the stone and wooden-beam cabin where his great-grandfather used to escape to drink bourbon, smoke cigars and swap stories with friends. The night was also leaving. The moon was a ghost. Still it would be sometime until the sun tinted pink the dew of the world's richest grass. The tent was standing, but the tables and the pavilion had been cleared of the remains of last night's party. Beyond rose the big house, white and old South. Reid saw a light in the kitchen, knew the coffee had been put on. But first he would check the horses. Always the horses.

It was quiet inside the stallion barn except for a few snorts, the paw of horseshoes against the straw-covered asphalt. In the distance, Reid heard the night guard's truck leaving one of the other barns, stop at the next, making rounds. Reid walked down the wide center lane, the memory of the night and the woman still washing over him. He moved toward the far end to a stall on the right, the brass nameplate on the bottom half of its Dutch door inscribed Aztec Treasure. A hot-blooded champion who would have been gelded had his genes not been worth gold. Reid was halfway down the corridor when he heard a low moan. He quickened his steps toward the almost human sound, already murmuring, "Easy, champ. What's the—"

His calming voice broke off as he met the horse's eyes, white, wet without tears. His first thought was colic. He went to open the door, frowning when he saw it hadn't been properly latched. He carefully slid back the solid slab of oak, nicked and deeply indented from the animal's frequent fits. The horse didn't rear up to claim his dominance as in the past. He only stared, his flanks heaving, his body trembling. Reid stepped toward the animal, then stopped, seeing the animal's foreleg held off the ground, dangling at the knee. He stared as if what he saw was not real, only more of the night's illusion. He felt the sweating horse's heat, his own heat of shock and fear. Finally he turned. And saw his brother's crumpled body lying in a bed of softest straw.

Chapter One

Dani touched a hard shoulder, a broad chest. Her hands were skilled, their touch delicate, her fingertips already knowing what would come. Softness, hardness, heat.

She stared into spiraling depths, dark eyes that drew her…frightened others. Such a complicated creature, this one. All male. Pure passion. Born to win.

She moved, and the eyes followed her. She saw the curve where light and dark met. A roll of white, a confession of what others didn't see—the colorless vulnerability.

Her lips touched the thin ridge between the watching eyes. A kiss to calm. Her hand caressed. The eyes watched.

"You won't even let 'em smell your sweat, will you, gorgeous?" The voice could have lulled lightning.

She squatted down, her hands skimming a lean leg.

"Tough guy. All day, dreaming only of a fast track, sweet fillies. That's all you want 'em to see, isn't it?"

Her hands cupped a twin leg of muscle and power. The proud male head turned. The eyes watched. "Yessir, they like to talk about you. Say you came out of the womb ready to fight, born bad. I say you never stood a chance. They knew who your father was." She stood, laid her cheek to silk. "Bloodlines."

She stepped back. "All this time we've been together, and still, you're giving me the show. Acting like you don't care. Breaking my heart."

Her hand followed a spine's curves. "But you're not fooling me, darlin'. Pretending not to care for nothing except ladies and long shots." Her hand paused. She leaned in, her voice almost inaudible. "You see I knew another like you."

She wrapped her arms around the thick neck of her current charge, felt the tremble beneath her cheek, the tremble in her heart. "Don't worry," she whispered into the dark softness. "You'll always be my favorite."

As she turned to leave, she felt the staying touch at the back of her neck, moving down to her hip. "A gullible girl would think you're returning the compliment."

She reached into her front pant pocket for the sought-after peppermint. "I, however, am not so naive."

She stepped outside the stall, surveying the shedrow. It was the height of August meet, and anyone who was anyone in the Thoroughbred racing world had brought the best of their stables to Saratoga for the month. Twisting the bill of her baseball cap to the back of her head, Dani looked up past the overhang of the unenclosed barn. The dawn mist had burned off to a bright blue that soothed rather than stunned the eyes, the heat comfortable enough to drink a Saratoga Sunrise and not get dizzy.

The horses had been walked, bathed, rubbed and brushed. Legs had been carefully checked for swelling, cuts or abrasions, then swabbed with poultices of medicated mud or iced and bandaged, if needed. Manes had been combed, feet painted, clover tossed into the straw bed and liquid vitamins poured over the second feeding of oats. Morning workouts were a mere memory.

It was past noon, and the air was shifting, becoming keener, closer, a held breath. The Thoroughbreds felt it. The muscles in their impossibly slender legs twitched. Their muzzles reared up, taking deep draughts of the charged air. Post time was coming.

Her chores done until it was time to fetch the evening feed and prepare the night bedding, Dani surveyed the shedrow, her body always instinctively angled toward the red-and-white striped roofs across the street.

A few other grooms sat outside the cinder block dorms, sipping beers, shooting the breeze, looking, too, without realizing it to the semicircle of the grandstand and the clubhouse, ever aware of the hundreds of dreams sitting beneath those wooden peaks. Dreams

that could die in a split second today, only to be res-
urrected tomorrow.

Behind her, Dani heard a voice feminine and falsely
drawling.

"Granddad told me the stink in here would smell
sweeter than the South in springtime one day."

Dani glanced over her shoulder and saw the stable
owner's granddaughter, Cicely Fox, breathe in, swelling her bosom as if serving it on a platter.

"But honey, stink is still stink." The blonde
laughed, tossing back her head. It was the movement
of purebreds. The jewels in her ears, the gold at her
throat and wrists caught the August light as she strut-
ted down the barn's dirt lane, steadying herself on the
arm of her cousin, Prescott.

"Watch where you step," Prescott advised as he
steered the woman to the right.

"O-o-o-o-oh!" Cicely squealed, sidestepping a trail
of fresh horse droppings.

Dani's gaze immediately went to the animals in
their stalls. They'd tense at much less than a woman's
whine. She heard rustling as several pawed the straw.
One nickered high. Another snorted. It sounded like a
laugh.

"You there. You there, boy."

It was a moment before Dani realized Prescott was
calling to her.

"Clean up that mess. This barn's not fit to walk
through."

Dani grabbed the shovel leaning against the rail, her
fingers curling tight on the handle but her "Yessir"

automatic. Once her reply might have been less abiding, but once she'd been young and reckless. No more. She knew her place, knew how dangerous it was to pretend otherwise.

"Goodness," Cicely drawled as she passed, shaking out several tissues from her purse and holding them to her upturned nose. "Such big ol' beautiful creatures." Her laughter was breathy, billowing the white cover. "But such big ol' nasties."

Moving toward the pile and out of earshot, Dani muttered, "I suppose yours smell like mint julep." She heard a low chuckle. Her body stiffened. When was she going to learn to be careful? She lifted her head, saw the man in the trainer's office door, a ghost of a smile remaining on his face as he met her gaze, sent her a silver wink. Her body flinched, seized by surprise. The face she looked at was as familiar as her own.

Reid Hamilton.

She looked away as if a shadowing bill of a baseball cap would save her. She steadied herself on the shovel, feeling his scrutiny, her incredulity. *Don't let him come closer.* If he came closer, touched her shoulder, spoke a familiar name, she would have to turn and look at him, the whites of her eyes signaling surrender.

She kept her head turned. She needed no study of this man. She knew that face too well—the high forehead, the abrupt angle of eyebrows, the overall excess of dark charm.

She heard him come near. She focused on a faraway

point, her breathing shallow, soundless, willing her body solid again.

"The man's blind, darling," he whispered in that soft Southern singsong. She felt his breath warm on her neck. Her head turned without permission. She saw the dark sheen of his crown as he bent over and picked up a cream-colored square from amid the straw and sprinkles of feed.

He handed her the piece of stationery. "I believe this is yours?"

She stared at the invitation in her hand. Saratoga Under the Stars—A Grand Gala. If he'd read the card, he would've known it no more belonged to her than the sun suddenly too hot all around her. Yet hadn't it been a night such as that five years ago? Didn't she still hear the men's sighs, their features soft with the last of boyhood, their hearts not yet hardened by disappointment or disbelief? Couldn't she still see the women's answering smiles as they'd watched, waited, wrapped in taffeta or silk, their beauty the very beat of the ball. Even now, she saw a young woman, a fine gentleman meeting, dancing, daring to draw close like undeniable dreams.

Dani closed her eyes, closed her heart. Who would think beyond these lowered lids such dreams were spun? Only she knew too well that desires rarely rely on reality. On the contrary, they seemed to delight in pairing the most unlikely alliances.

She opened her eyes, raised her head and met the man's silver gaze. She shook her head, held out the invitation to Cicely watching them several stalls over.

Cicely stepped closer to look at the card. She unsnapped her purse and looked inside. "It must've fallen out when I got a tissue." She eyed the invitation. "It was on the ground?"

"Yes, Miss Fox."

Cicely's hand reached out, then retreated. "Throw it away." She tossed her head as she turned to her cousin and laughed lightly. "I think they'll let me in, don't you?"

Her smile turned inviting as she shifted her gaze to the gray-eyed man. "We should all go together."

Dani looked up from the embossed square straight into the man's silver study. His face wore new lines but still the skin stretched too tight over raw bones. The glints of light in his eyes were gone, leaving shadow. She wasn't the only one who had suffered.

She didn't look away. It was too late. She couldn't risk the naked movement. Her eyes ached. Her heart ached. She pushed back the cap from her head, freeing the brown hair beneath, freeing the man who had known her only one night. One night when she'd been a mystery unraveling. Red-haired and reckless. And he had not resisted.

Now she turned her head, not the elegant toss of wellborn women, but a wrenching movement. She felt the fine hairs along her nape pulling, her skin straining beneath her chin where first it would begin to slacken. The movement was too abrupt, but she had no choice. If she stared at the man one moment longer, her eyes would lock as her heart had locked all those years ago.

Cicely's hand reached out again, not for the invitation but for the gray-eyed man. The linen-smooth palm beckoned. Dani felt the heat of the man's gaze. She stared at Cicely's offered hand as if those ivory fingers would rise and bless them all. *Take it, take it,* she urged. Her thoughts could have been words said aloud as the man moved toward Cicely, her hand slipping into the curve of his arm and pulling him close.

"We'll pop in, have a few drinks, then be on our way," Cicely said as her escorts matched her steps. She snuggled closer between the two men.

Reid didn't hear the soprano chatter beside him. He was thinking of the woman behind him. At first, he'd only seen her bare profile, the check of her jaw, the muscles working in her throat. It was when she'd looked up, the slopes of her face becoming less neutral, the feminine more forceful, he'd thought he'd seen something else. Something familiar. He had smiled at her mumbled comment; inside he had mocked himself and his own foolish obsession.

Still, she seemed familiar in a vague, indistinct way like an image not quite formed that nagged and tugged at odd hours. He might have even looked over his shoulder once more if he hadn't seen the lank length of her tarnished hair. The woman he thought of, the woman he always thought of had hair violent red and surely, wouldn't be found mucking out stalls. Still… His head turned without thought. She hadn't moved.

Dani clenched the shovel handle, only the brace of muscle up her arm staying her. *Go,* she ordered unspoken until the man looked forward once more. She grasped her shovel and watched him, watched him go, the powder puff of a woman beside him. She dropped her gaze, seeking respite. She saw Cicely's tiny feet stepping in thin leather straps, made for the most refined of arches. The shoes' heels, high and equally thin, tipped the soles up, lightly muscled the calves. The stockinged legs shimmered like a heat wave, stretching up to a fitted flamingo pink skirt topped with a jacket. Dani had always hated the color pink.

The trio moved farther down the row of boxes. She was safe. Even if Reid looked back again, he would still see only a woman brown and beige and dusty as the hay and dirt beneath her boots. She watched, made herself watch and felt the thin cotton of her T-shirt stick to her back.

The three stopped before the stall Dani had left only minutes ago. "Here's the one you saw," Prescott said.

The dark colt's ears pivoted. He raised his head, arched his neck high above the metal half gate. Reid stared. The animal was the image of its sire. A Kentucky Derby winner who had run like the Devil and behaved twice as bad. A champion who went crazy one night, killing a man and himself.

Reid stood before that stallion's son now. Cicely started to speak, but Reid's hand hushed her. Her cousin tapped her shoulder, silently gestured, and they stepped away. Reid stayed.

Dani watched him. She knew he was remembering that night. They'd said he'd discovered them—his brother's battered body on the straw, the magnificent horse, his right foreleg shattered. Before there had been only dancing and desire. Afterward, only death.

Reid kept his gaze on the colt as he spoke to Prescott. "They predicted he'd end his first season as one of the top two-year-olds. What happened?"

Prescott stepped toward the stall. "You know what they say—'if he didn't have bad luck, he wouldn't have any luck at all.' That's what you're looking at right now. Began with a lung infection that cut his training short. Then recurring bouts of colic took their toll. Even still, he had broken his maiden and placed in an allowance when he acted up while being washed, slipped and cracked his pelvis. We rested him for nine months. He fought us the whole time. Some horses you'd never see on the dirt again after that, but this one, he lives to run." Prescott looked at the horse but didn't reach out his hand to stroke him. The horse didn't offer himself to the man. "He's got the breeding and the bone, but he can be a brute."

Reid's stare stayed level with the animal. "You didn't cut him." The horse tossed his head and snorted.

"Granddad believes if he can just score some points on the track, his real worth will be as a stallion, but so far he hasn't rallied. After three starts here, he's still the long shot. Until he can show us he can find the winner's circle, we're not entering him in anything but test drives." The man eyed the dark animal. The colt dipped his huge head, butted the stall guard.

Prescott shook his head. "Won one ungraded race in his career yet he's already famous for being one big hassle. Our trainer says sell him or geld him and I agree but Granddad can be as stubborn as this colt.

Probably why he's got a soft spot for him. But after these last performances, even he's ready to throw in the towel. If we ever get this colt to the breeding shed, between his record and his temperament, the fees will never come to what we hoped."

Reid listened to the other man, his gaze locked with the colt's. He turned away without saying anything.

"Shall we wait for your mother here?" Cicely asked Reid as the two men joined her. "She's meeting us, isn't she?"

"She'll be along. She was just going to stop by the Woodhouse Stables on the way over."

The three walked to the end of the row and stepped out from the overhang into the sun, the light catching at Cicely's gold and gems. Dani threw the invitation on the pile of manure and angled her shovel.

She was stopped by a frantic yell. Turning toward the cry, she saw a child come from around the corner of the opposite stables and shoot across the dirt circle between the two barns. An older woman, still yelling, followed in pursuit but she was no match for the child's swift feet. Laughing, the child zigzagged around an overturned bucket, under a sawhorse and started up the row of stalls.

Dani waited until he was almost past her, then ducking beneath the rail, caught the child by the arm.

"Whoa there," she said in the same voice she used to calm the horses. Still the boy squirmed to get away. She wrapped both her arms around him and lifted him up, bracing his wiggling body against her chest. He locked his legs around her and arched back so naturally she didn't have time to stop him. He was hanging upside down and laughing once more, so free and full of glee, she found herself chuckling even as she tightened her arms and pulled him upward. They met face to laughing face. She saw the child's silver eyes. It could have been her own soul staring back at her.

Chapter Two

"Good God, boy, you'll give your grandmother and I both a heart attack one of theses days."

Dani looked up to the voice, saw the same silver circles.

"Sorry." The blood was beginning to come back into Reid's face. "He's four. And hell on wheels. I swear I'm going to have to attach a shank line to his shorts."

"Four," Dani repeated in a quiet voice. Her gaze went to the boy.

The child nodded and held up four fingers.

She smiled. The ache multiplied, moved across her skin.

"I've trained thousand-pound animals." Reid shook his head. "But forty pounds of four-year-old..." He looked at the boy, his eyes soft as a night she remembered.

"They're a special breed." She almost touched the child's hair, the same color as hers when she'd been a child.

Reid reached for the boy. "I'm afraid being raised by an overindulgent uncle and a doting grandmother doesn't help the situation."

Uncle? She didn't mean to tighten her grip on the boy. "He's not your son?"

The surprise in her voice caused Reid to look at her. She straightened her arms to give him the boy, still not sure she could let go.

"He's my brother's boy."

No! She almost denied it aloud. Reid still studied her. She steeled her expression while emotions sliced through her: confusion, guilt, yearning, hope. She let go of the child.

Reid settled the boy on one hip. His gaze stayed on her. She faced him, her features purposely bland, her insides twisting. She'd been so sure.

"My brother died several years ago. There was an accident."

She knew. "I'm sorry."

"I'm the boy's legal guardian."

It made sense, she told herself. Perfect sense. Until she looked at the boy's profile.

"He must give you and your wife a run for your money." The words were out of her mouth before she could stop them. She had to know.

"No wife." Reid looked at the boy. "Just you and me. Right, bub?"

"Right, bub," the boy repeated.

Dani watched the man and child. It was like a dream.

"If you can teach the Thoroughbreds to run like

that, you'll make a fortune in this business one day."
Reid's tone became stern. "Until then, Trey Adam
Hamilton III, the barns aren't your personal play-
ground."

She heard the name. Reid's brother's name.

"Understand?"

The boy nodded.

"Okay then." Reid lifted the boy, swung him up
on his shoulders.

The child wrapped his arms beneath Reid's chin,
crouched low over the man's crown. "Rider up."

Reid smiled as he caught the boy's hands in his
own. "It's in the blood, I'm afraid." The boy bucked
up and down on his shoulders.

Dani stared at the child, wondering whose blood ran
through those tender veins.

"An obvious champion," she said. She didn't realize she was hanging on to the hem of the boy's
shorts until she gave it an affectionate tug. She looked
down and saw the strawberry-colored mark on the
child's thigh. Her fingers gripped the material. The
first time she'd seen that thick V-shape, she'd thought
it had looked like a bird in flight. She had to let go.

"Are you fellas ready?" Cicely called. Dani forced
her fingers to drop, her gaze to shift from the boy to
where Cicely stood, fanning Georgia Hamilton. "Your
mother, Reid, needs a beverage," Cicely said.

"Just gathering my guy here," Reid told her.

The child rested his chin on the Reid's crown,
looked down at Dani. "Celery," he pronounced.

"Cicely," Reid corrected, trying not to smile. He

lost. Still smiling, he looked at Dani. "Thank you." Moving one hand up to support the boy, he extended his other hand to Dani in gratitude. Her hand touched his, withdrew before his fingers found hers.

"Trey," Reid instructed, his silver eyes still on Dani. "Thank the nice lady for reining you in."

Twin silver eyes looked down into hers. "Thanks, nice lady."

She touched his bare sweet knee. "Any time."

The boy looked down at her and smiled. How often had she imagined what he looked like, how his laughter sounded, what he would feel like in her arms? Her hand stayed on the child.

"Thank you again," Reid said. "Say goodbye, Trey."

"Bye," the child told her.

"Goodbye." Dani let go, clasping her hands behind her back to hide their tremble.

SHE FOUND her father sitting between Willie and Lou at the bar that served the huge blue margaritas. It was early. The night was maybe only two or three rounds old.

He looked up, meeting her reflection in the mirror behind the bar. His hair had grayed at the temples, and there was bloat beneath the eyes from alcohol and age, but overall, the face so many women had found handsome hadn't changed. *Good genes* he would say. Bloodlines.

He tapped his cigarette against the ashtray's edge. "Sit down. Have a sip with me and the boys here. I'm going to tell them about the day I rubbed a Derby winner."

"C'mon, Mick, don't you have any new stories?" Willie raised his beer to his smiling lips. Dani's reflection in the mirror stayed grave.

Mick pushed his empty glass toward the edge of the bar, signaling the bartender. He was a man who believed a life of excess was the only life worth living. It was often the secret to his appeal. One day it would kill him.

"Some stories deserve repeating. The home stretch at Churchill Downs is one of them, right, love?" Mick met his daughter's eyes in the mirror.

"I need to talk to you."

Mick took a sip from the full tumbler the bartender put down in front of him and studied his daughter in the mirror's reflection. "Let the ol' man buy you a drink first, Dani girl. You're getting as high-strung as the ponies."

She felt the tension in her limbs, the jerk in her pulse. "No." One syllable but it sounded of a madness in the making.

Her father swiveled slowly, his drink wrapped in one hand. Lou and Willie studied their beers. Mick studied her. She smelled the whiskey in his glass, on his breath. She should wait for a few more rounds when the liquor loosened his tongue. She thought of the child. She couldn't wait.

"I saw Reid Hamilton today."

Her father looked at her a long second. He swiveled back to the bar, avoiding her mirrored gaze. He stubbed out his cigarette long after it stopped smoking. Just as she decided he was going to ignore her or try to escape, he raised his gaze and gave her a long look in the mirror. With an exhale part breath, part sigh, he slid off the stool and gestured grandly to the square tables in the back. "Let's have a seat, shall we?"

Sipping from his drink, he led the way. He was shorter than her, but his build was as narrow and taut. In his youth, he'd dreamed of wearing the silks, but the dream and the paddock were as close as he'd ever come.

Father and daughter sat down, facing one another. Dani's hand clenched into a ball on the scarred tabletop. She covered it with her other hand, her fingers curling, pressing into the thin flesh, slim bones. She had too much at risk to fall apart now.

"I saw Reid Hamilton today."

Mick's gaze shifted for a second, then came back to her. He took a long drink. His eyes watched her above the rim. She squeezed her hands together.

"So you've said." He set his glass carefully on the wet ring that had formed on the wood.

She should've waited. Waited until the whiskey had made him brash. She'd been in too much of a hurry. Reckless.

"He had a child with him. A boy."

She watched for his reaction. He reached out, his fingertips touching the cool sides of the glass.

"He said it was his nephew. His brother's boy."

Her father drew circles on the glass's damp surface.

"I held the child in my arms."

Her father's hand went still. He lifted his fingers, touched the wetness to his lips.

Dani's hands clutched each other as if to snap bone. "I held the child in my arms."

Her father raised his glass to his lips. "Dani." He stopped, said no more. He drank.

Her voice was eerily even. "Reid Hamilton isn't the boy's uncle. He's his father."

Mick pulled out a pack of cigarettes, tapped one out and lit it, his eyes narrowing. "You said the child is the brother's boy."

"The child is Reid Hamilton's son." The words bubbled up, burned her throat "He has a son." She'd become a broken record.

"He has a son. My son." It wasn't a question. She wouldn't ask. She wouldn't let it be denied.

"Dani." She heard pity in her father's voice. The drum of her blood became louder.

"He's my son. I saw him. I held him." Her hands unclenched, reached out, pleading.

Mick exhaled. The stale smells of smoke and liquor came, clung to her. He tapped the cigarette on the ashtray's edge. "That's it? You held the boy in your arms and you decide he's your child?" He kept tapping the cigarette after the ashes had fallen.

"The boy looks like Mom." Her father stiffened, reached for his drink. "He looks like you."

He set down the drink. His hand stayed curled around the glass. "Then he'll have good luck with the ladies, but why would that make the boy your child?"

She looked away from the reasonableness in her father's face.

"Reid Hamilton himself said the boy was his nephew." Mick adopted a patient tone. "Why would he say that if it weren't so?"

"You will have to tell me that. Tell me." Her hand reached out, gripped her father's hand holding the drink. Liquor sloshed over the sides of the glass. "Tell me."

With that awful patronizing expression still on his face, her father pulled a fresh linen handkerchief from his pant pocket. No paper tissues for Mick Tate. Always a clean handkerchief, snow-white and starched. He ironed them himself. He had dried her tears with them. He now patted the whiskey off her hand.

"Today you saw Reid Hamilton with a child." His tone stayed patient. "A child who's about the same age as—"

She pulled her hand away. "I didn't say anything about the child's age."

"No, but I'm guessing the boy isn't five-foot-six and starting to shave or you wouldn't have assumed he was your son, would you?" He smiled indulgently.

"He's four. And he is my son." She heard the plea in her voice and was ashamed.

"Dani, listen to me, five years ago, you weren't much more than a child yourself."

Five years ago. Her eighteenth birthday. Her father had been determined to mark the occasion. He had arranged the car, the dress, the engraved invitation that got her past the gate into Georgia Hamilton's legendary pre-Derby dinner dance. She wouldn't have been surprised if he'd strung the extra stars that seemed to light the sky that night over Hamilton Hills.

She stared at the man opposite her. His whole life Mick Tate had been trying to make fairy tales come true. That one night he had succeeded.

Three months later the pregnancy test had showed positive. Dani had stopped believing in fairy tales.

"What you did was the right thing to do." Her father's voice brought her back. "It was a brave thing."

"To give my child up?" Pain sliced into her.

"To give your child more." Mick lifted the cigarette to his lips, drawing deep, watching her. He picked up his drink. "Let me tell you what happened. Today you saw Reid Hamilton with a child about the same age as your baby would be, and it all became a bit too real. Much, much too real. Now the guilt gnaws at you. That's what happened. Conscience." He cradled his glass, looking into the amber liquid. "Such a liability."

The waitress came to their table. Her father drained the glass and handed it to her. "Another double, darling. How 'bout you, Dani girl? Ready for that drink?"

She shook her head. Mick shrugged his shoulders and smiled at the waitress, watched the woman walk away. Dani studied her father's profile. At one time, he could make her believe anything. It had been his charm. And her undoing.

He turned to her, saw her study. "You did the right thing, love. It's no life for a child."

"You didn't give me up." She spoke quietly.

"No, but after your mother died, I had Nanny to look after you until she got sick. By that time, you were old enough to come with me. Still, don't think I wouldn't have sent you to your mother's family if they would have had you. Sons of bitches. With their fat bank accounts and their precious reputations, thinking they can pick and choose their kin like ordering from a Chinese menu." He reached for the drink no longer there, the burn of anger and alcohol in his eyes. "No, I didn't give you up. I was too damn selfish. But that doesn't mean I didn't want more for you than bouncing from track to track, living in roach boxes, hoping for a triple to get us out of last week's hole."

The waitress returned and set the drink on the table. Mick lifted the glass, gave the woman a wink and took a long swallow. He put the glass down, the look he gave the liquor more appreciative than the one granted the waitress.

"Believe me…" He leaned back too far in his chair. He teetered for a moment, then steadied. "Your child has more."

She looked at this man who had brought her to a magical place where horses flew and money multiplied and her mother had always laughed long and full while bits of betting slips floated through the air like confetti. "My baby had a birthmark. A small V-shape on his right thigh. The boy with Reid today has the same mark. He's my child."

Her father looked down, studied the liquor.

"He's my child." She waited. A song started to play on the jukebox. Sudden laughter across the room made her jump, but at their table, there was only silence.

"A blood test will prove it."

Her father looked up, studied her. "I did it for the boy." He looked away. "I did it for you."

She sat perfectly still, fearing one wrong word, one revealing movement, and he'd stop. Her father took a drink, and then another until when he set the glass down, his hand didn't shake anymore. She held her breath, the blood humming in her head.

"You were in trouble. I was always in trouble. You know all that." His hand waved a dismissal before reaching for his cigarettes. "We both wanted to give the child more. The Hamiltons could give him more. He's growing up well taken care of, never wanting. Plus these people aren't strangers. They're his real family. He's with his father, for Pete's sake." Mick took a quick drink.

"Reid doesn't even know the boy is his son." The truth was worse in her own thin voice.

"If he'd known the child was his, he might've tried to find out who the mother was. I wanted to protect you."

"He didn't know who I was that night. No one did."

"What if he'd decided to find out? What if he'd found out the mother of his child wasn't some mysterious Southern deb but the gal who mucked out the shedrow stalls?"

It was true. She'd deceived Reid first.

Mick gestured, the ash falling off his cigarette on

to the scarred table. "We're talking the Bluegrass, darling. Where people are assessed just like the horses—by their pedigree. You know that." He drank, the liquor going down faster. His glass hit the table too hard. "You know that."

She watched him raise his empty glass as the waitress passed nearby. He'd never forgiven her mother's family for not believing he'd loved their daughter. They'd thought he was after her money. But he had loved her. He loved her still.

He set the glass on the waitress's tray, turned back to Dani. "I wasn't going to see this child treated like the dung they tiptoe past on their way to the box seats."

She wanted to protest Reid wouldn't be like that, but she had no right. If she'd been sure, she would have gone to him when she first found out she was pregnant. She hadn't. An elegant illusion named Danielle DeVries had bewitched Reid that night. The reality was a stable groom named Dani Tate. Once he had learned of her deception, why would he have had anything to do with her?

"The tests from the grandmother's blood proved the boy was family, and that's all they wanted to know. Now he'll grow up a Hamilton. As he should." Dani knew if her father had a drink, he would've raised it in a toast.

"Plus the price on the offspring of a dead son would be much higher, wouldn't it?"

She'd surprised him, catching him before he could school his expression. She loved her father but she knew his flaws. She felt a whirling in her empty stomach and was afraid she was going to be sick.

He masked his surprise, lit a fresh cigarette, looked to see if the waitress was coming. "I was in trouble. You know that."

Yes, she'd known that. They'd gone south the next day. Kentucky had always been home, but her father and she worked the East Coast circuit, their location usually dependent on how many miles her father needed between himself and the bookies he owed. Eventually things would cool off or her father would hit enough daily doubles to go home to Kentucky. They had been on their way to Florida when Dani had heard about the accident at Hamilton Hills. She had been working at Hialeah Park when she'd learned she was pregnant. After the baby was born, she'd run, working the circuit west to Santa Anita Park, then up north to Portland Meadows, never staying too long in any one spot. Eventually she'd circled back to the East, settling on Fox Run Farm in upstate New York. She'd never gone back to the Bluegrass.

"I had the lawyer who handled the arrangements only ask for what I needed. Not a penny extra." Her father's drink arrived. The drone of blood in Dani's head became louder. She watched him take a long sip. He leaned back, laced his fingers together like a reasonable man. "What's fair is fair."

"You sold your own grandson." She spoke from the pain and sorrow that always ran through her sparse veins.

His hand slapped the table. "It wasn't like that."

He leaned forward, lowered his voice. "You couldn't give the boy the life he deserved. I did."

There was the rush of blood in her head, the sour taste in her mouth, and the terrible truth. She stood up too fast, her chair scraping the faded floor.

"Where are you going?"

She looked blindly at her father, shook her head. She didn't know. She was working on instinct now.

"Dani, sit down. Listen to me." His calm tone only made the confusion inside her worse. She gripped the chair. Her father's eyes were bright from whiskey but his speech was still clear, his stare steady. "You wanted your child to have the best, and he does. He's safe and he's loved."

"He's healthy, too. And handsome." She heard her own anguish. She looked away, her gaze darting about the dim room, unable to look directly at anything. The deep, frantic mix of emotions inside her threatened. She closed her eyes, afraid to make any movement at all. When she opened them, she saw the brightness in her father's eyes had become moist, brilliant.

"You need a drink, Dani."

"I don't need a drink."

"Something to eat." She heard the caring.

She shook her head.

"You're tired. Go get a good night's rest."

"I don't want to sleep. I don't want to eat. I don't want to drink." She hung on to the edge of the chair, her knees buckling, her strength gone. Pain and longing were the only life left inside her.

"I want my baby."

SHE WENT HOME. Not to the small anonymous room in town she'd rented with her percent of recent winnings, but to the only home she'd ever known. The night guard waved her through without a glance at the employee tag she wore around her neck. It wasn't the first time he'd seen her here after hours.

She parked in the almost empty lot and cut across the gravel and grass to the barns. The cinder block dormitories were dark. The 4:00 a.m. feeding always came too fast.

The shedrow was sleeping. Lights were minimal—the silent flare of a solitary cigarette; subtle security lights turned the night from black to gray; the wink of fireflies.

She walked on, the turf yielding, the gravel, graveyard gray. All paths led to the track. All ended at the winner's circle. She breathed in the incense of unspoken dreams, the sweat of loss, the rare sweet sachet of success.

Home.

Where the stakes were high. And second chances few.

One stumble and it could be over. She'd seen it happen as recently as last Thursday in the fourth. Maybe it was the sloppy track? Maybe it was a small hole, a bad step? Who knows? One minute a thousand-pound machine is barreling toward glory; the next, a winch is pulling its carcass across the finish line.

She followed the bend of the training track, seeing horses and riders where there were none.

A son. Her son. She grabbed the track's outside rail

and held fast. In a world where second chances were rare, she knew she'd been given a gift.

She walked the track's perimeter, circling with the phantoms of those who'd tried and won and those who'd tried and lost. It had been a night much blacker than this when her knees had pulled up and her body had clenched and pain at first not much more than a woman's weeping had become a storm. Her legs had split, and she had stopped breathing, stopped thinking, stopped feeling until there was a rush of warmth and a wail of life to match her own. The night had ended then. The darkness had lifted and, in a haze, she'd seen a blood-streaked bundle, white and pink and so pretty, she'd held out her hands. They'd laid him naked on her breast. It wasn't enough. She'd asked for a little more time. They'd brought him to her washed and wrapped in blankets. She'd inspected every inch of that tiny body, memorizing, promising not to forget, trying to explain. She fell asleep, cradling him in her arms. He'd been gone when she awoke. She'd never touched her baby again.

Until today.

Her hands held each other now as she walked with the night's ghosts. She had no rights, she knew that. She had relinquished all claims. She would never demand anything—not family or love or forgiveness. She would ask for nothing from the child or his father. But would it be so wrong to be near, to watch the child grow from a toddler to a boy to a man? Invisible, silent, watching, protecting, she would be no more than the specters surrounding her now. Surely it wasn't asking too much?

Her father was right. The child had a home, a family, a name. She would do nothing to jeopardize that. She would ask for nothing, expect nothing. She had no rights.

But she'd given her son up once. She wouldn't give him up again.

Now was the one moment Reid knew peace—when the morning was dawn, soft and moist and warm as the steam rising from the barrels of water heating in the backstretch. When all the world was vague and muffled—the hooves on the turf, the talk between the trainers huddled at the rail, watching their charges. It wouldn't last long. The mist would break, and the horses, the people would no longer be illusions in the lavender August light. Everything would become real once more, and Reid would remember that what was one minute could be gone the next. A turn of the head, a chance look and whole lives could change. But, for now, moving though the morning haze, he might have been dreaming.

He joined his trainer, Smiley Woods, at the rail. Smiley had trained two of Hamilton Hills' three Derby champions, and Reid knew the man would be welcome at any farm he choose. He'd even told him so when Hamilton Hills' financial state became public, and the offers for Smiley's services began pouring in. But Smiley had only shook his head and said, ''This is where I belong.'' Such was the spell Hamilton Hills could cast.

Reid nodded now to the one man he still trusted, then turned his attention back to the horse coming down the lane.

''What do you think?''

The horse trotted by, his ears pinned, his hind end bouncing, pulling so hard at the reins, his rider was gritting his teeth. ''He's a bombshell.''

About a hundred yards away, the animal reared up, but the exercise boy was ready for him and kicked him forward. A few lengths down the rail, the Fox Run Farm trainer leaned out over the rail and shouted, ''Contain him.''

Smiley watched the horse head for the turn. He was a mammoth man with a perpetual scowl that had earned him his nickname. But despite his size and scowl, there was a constant calm around him. The horses had taught him to walk slowly and speak softly.

''I knew a gelding once who moved like that in the back end, and he—''

He broke off, a life at the racetrack having schooled him in superstitions and jinxes. ''I would want to see some X rays,'' was all he'd say.

Reid watched the dark colt, long-legged, tight-bellied, all reckless desire to run, and although a healthy respect for curses and hexes wouldn't permit either man to say this aloud, both knew what they saw as the dark horse shot past them. It could have been Aztec Treasure flying across the soft soil.

''He's a stall walker.'' Smiley's gaze never left the

colt. "Guard told me he had a fit last night, pawing at the door and snorting, running in circles as if already on the track. The vets leave him to last. He'll take a nip as soon as your head is turned. Imagine he likes to kick too, but the groom who's with him now has been with him through the infections and the fracture, and they say he's almost playful with her."

They watched the animal go wide, grinding his bit, fighting the rider.

"Horse does love to run though."

Reid looked at the trainer, saw his rare smile of secret delight reserved solely for Thoroughbreds and Kentucky bourbon.

Smiley looked at his stopwatch, then back at the horse. "Some that ornery are just mean or maybe scared. This one though, he thinks he's superior. You can see it in his eyes. There's no wildness there or fear. Just one hundred percent insolence."

"His dam was Every Bit A Lady. Good grass mare. Had some success in the New York stakes."

Smiley nodded. "As steady as they come."

"This one though—he's up, he's down. The Foxes have about written him off as one big mistake."

Smiley silently studied the horse.

"He's running in a claimer tomorrow."

The large man glanced over. "And I thought you came up to Saratoga for all the high society hoopla?"

Reid returned the other man's wry smile. Both knew the invitations had been few after the accident and the investigation. Those that did come now went unanswered.

Smiley looked back across the oval. "But, here you are, scouting for salvation."

Reid followed his trainer's gaze. They'd both seen it happen before. One horse. That's all that was needed. A few healthy purses on the track, then an enviable income earned in the breeding shed for a good number of years. One horse.

The two men stood so close, their elbows hit as they leaned on the rail and watched the horse run, tail streaming straight out, nose, neck, back all aligned, born like hope, to go forward.

"He's had a few setbacks, hasn't been able to get his performance back up. They wanted him to have some impressive runs before they turned him out to stud. He only started one season before he was way-laid with ailments. I'm betting he's got a few wins in him."

Smiley, as always, watched the horse. "I'll give you my best."

It was the closest thing to a promise at the track.

"I'll work with you on this one." Reid saw the trainer slip him a glance. "We should have enough time until the rains come. If they do come early, I'll ship him south the last few weeks, but I'll go with him."

"You taking this one personal, huh?"

The horse went by at a walk now. The rider exited the track, steering the animal toward the barns.

"It's always personal."

The animal's head swung from side to side and his ears lay flat as he fought being reined in. Reid headed toward the colt, following the winded, damp horse as if already assured redemption.

The colt's ears were still pinned when they reached the barns. A female groom giving a leg up to a rider watched the horse's return, then crossed the soft dirt toward the animal. She was thin with the lean frame that comes from excessive work or excessive worry. Her face was unadorned and her hair in the single simple braid of a young girl. But as she moved toward the animal, Reid saw beneath her straight legged denims and loose T-shirt, the fullness of breasts, the curves of hips, the body of a woman.

"Get the hose for this one," the rider warned as he dismounted. "He'll never stand still for the sponge."

The groom reached behind the horse's head and scratched him on the spot of the withers where horses can't reach. Reid saw the animal's head turn to look at the diminutive woman. The colt's ears pricked forward.

"He'll let me know," the groom replied. "He's the boss."

Reid moved toward the horse as the woman took something from her pocket, offered it in her palm to the animal. "A peppermint, a carrot or two, and he's a lamb," she told the rider as the horse nuzzled her palm. "He just likes to remind you of who he is."

She looked even smaller next to the beast she still soothed. She stroked the horse's heaving side. Her movements were unhurried, reassuring, the quiet, consistent gestures of hands that had given care their whole life.

"They tell me you're the only groom he'll have." Reid moved closer to the horse.

She looked up, meeting his gaze. He had heard the soft Kentucky in her drawl but there was more, something else vague but still familiar. He looked into the pale green of her eyes, clear as water, and, for a moment, was disoriented. She turned her head away, her long braid swinging forward, falling over her shoulder, across the rise of her breast. There was the warmth of the animal between them and the lingering uneasy confusion created by the woman's profile. Then Reid remembered. She was the woman who'd caught his nephew yesterday when the boy had run wild across the backside.

"We've met, haven't we?"

Chapter Three

He saw fear in her pale green eyes. He hadn't meant to frighten her. He knew it wasn't de rigueur for the owners and jockeys to talk to the grooms. The track was divided into two worlds—the racing set and the training set. He, however, had always lived in both and even if he hadn't, wouldn't have abided such a distinction.

"Yesterday, here at the stables." He smiled to put the woman at ease. Those light green eyes looked at him. "Weren't you the one who corralled my nephew? Little guy?" He measured a height of about three feet with his hands. "Faster than the speed of light?"

She nodded, but didn't return his smile.

He stepped back, observing once more the animal's conformation, the legs, etched, muscular columns stacked straight and clean. Looking at them alone was a pleasure.

"How is he?" the groom asked.

He looked at her. Her beauty was quiet. A man wouldn't see it at the first glance nor probably the second, but if he was wise enough to look a third time as Reid did now, he would wonder how he'd missed it before. "Who?" he asked.

"The boy." She looked away from him as she spoke, busied herself removing the saddle. The horse swung his head toward him.

"Sleeping I hope, but that's a long shot. Odds are he's already up, pestering his grandmother for a Moon Pie."

"A Moon Pie?" The groom paused, the horse's tack in her arms. "In the morning?"

Reid stepped forward and took the tack from her with such a natural movement, she didn't object until it was no longer in her hands. He ignored her protests, hoisting the tack higher and marveling at the small woman's strength. "His favorite breakfast. I don't doubt he gets it now and again when I'm safely out of sight. My mother spoils him rotten."

As he turned from the tack stand, he saw the girl's lips curve and knew he'd put her at ease. She had a lovely full-lipped smile. He smiled back at her. "How long have you groomed for this outfit?"

"Almost two years."

He nodded toward the horse. "You took care of him when he fractured his pelvis?"

"And when he had the lung infection, the colic." Her smile disappeared, leaving a sudden maturity in her face far beyond her years.

"No wonder he trusts you. You've stuck by him."

"He's just had a bit of bad luck is all." The colt

shuffled. She caressed the animal's neck in silent communication. "That doesn't mean you abandon him."

A cloud came across the woman's features and her eyes darkened to the green of May. She turned, led the horse to a waiting pail of soapy water.

"Loyalty. I like that." Reid thought of the innuendo following his brother's death and Aztec Treasure's fatal injury. The investigation had eventually ruled the incident an accident, but most said that was only because there was no evidence to prove otherwise. Reid still heard the whispers when he walked into a room.

"Obviously so does he," Reid noted as the horse rested his nose on the woman's shoulder.

The woman didn't look at him as she began the colt's bath. Reid sensed he had made her uncomfortable again. He should go, let her do her work. Still he stood, watching her slip the sponge rhythmically across withers to loins, the steam rising from the colt's flanks.

"You just have to pay him a little attention now and then. Everybody is too quick to forget who he is." She rinsed the horse. "But he knows exactly who he is."

She finished putting on the cold-water bandages and blanketed the colt. "A winner," she said quietly as she watched the horse being led away by a hot walker. She looked directly at Reid. "It's his meanness they talk about but it's his heart they'll remember."

Reid saw in her expression she loved the animal as only grooms could—with the bonds of a mother to a child. He understood. He himself was drawn to the colt. He looked at the horse being hand-walked and knew there was something that colt could give him. A dream.

He turned back to the woman. The sensation remained as if she, too, had the answers to endless questions. The sense of familiarity returned, stronger this time, obviously fostered by their shared fondness for the horse being led around and around the walking ring.

The groom glanced up and saw his study. She busied herself cleaning up, uncomfortable once more. He should go. His own reluctance surprised him. He picked up the pail for her. Her hand shot out, grabbed the pail's handle.

"Thank you." She squared her feet, made her stance firm but he saw from her inability to hold his gaze, she was ill at ease. He let go of the bucket.

"Goodbye..." Funny he should feel such an intimacy, yet he didn't even know her name.

"Goodbye." She set the pail down and squatted, pretending to tighten her shoelaces. Out of the corners of her eyes, she watched him walk away. She thought about the boy. She wouldn't let herself think about the man, the way even now her breath came hot and thick. She could only think about the boy. Nothing else.

Saratoga's closing day was next Monday, Labor Day. Many of the outfits were packing up this weekend, moving on to Belmont Park, then south for the winter. Dani was going south, too, but not with Solstice and the Fox Run team. She was going home to Kentucky and the Keeneland Racecourse, only fields away from Hamilton Hills. She hadn't told anyone. She had to tell the colt first. The horse already knew something was changing. He'd been edgy, walking the stall more, dancing with a jump in the air on his front legs and two or three head tosses. She had to tell him today.

She saw the walker leading the animal back, a look in the horse's eye as if he were listening to something far away, something humans could never hear or see. She took the lead line, murmured, "There, now," heard the tenderness in her voice.

She led him into his freshly-bedded stall, he always seeming too big for his box. The late summer light found the straw and turned it blond. She picked up the hard brush and the currycomb, and as she rubbed, she explained everything in a low voice that now held a clef of sadness. She found the soft brush and began to alternate a hard stroke with a soft one, the rhythm matching her murmurs of hope and fear, and her hands dully cramping.

She crouched to the side, running her hand down the front of the legs, feeling for the heat or swelling that signaled hurting. "Staying away isn't a choice, you see. In fact, there is no choice. All right, yes, some will say there's always a choice, and in my head, I know that."

She rubbed the legs with a mix of alcohol and liniment. "But in my heart, there is no choice. I have to go. Or it will be like giving him up all over again." She wrapped the legs with clean white cotton from the ankle to just below the knee and then wrapped them

again with flannel, careful they were tight enough to
stay but not too tight to cause the legs to fill with fluid.
"I'm only going to be nearby, you see. Not close
enough to cause any trouble but close enough to get
a glimpse or two, watch him grow. God, you should
see him. Maybe you did. Yesterday. Right here at the
barns. Yesterday. I held him in my arms."

She fell silent so the shake in her hands would stop,
and she could fasten the last steel pin.

She straightened, unfastened the tethered horse, removed his halter. "I have to go, Solstice. He's my
child, you see."

She turned, bent to move the feed tub, when she felt
a breath along the left curve of her neck and then, the
sharp edges of teeth closing around her ear. She didn't
move. Neither did the horse. A slight bearing down
and her ear would be his. A long second went by. The
pressure along her flesh stayed the same, not hard
enough to cut the flesh but tight enough to hold on.
Another second passed. She heard the scratching of
another groom raking outside. She stood with the perfect stillness that had bonded her to this horse. As soon
as they'd met, she'd recognized the animal's need for
a space to call on and always find calm. After that,
when he had come to her and butted her shoulder or
nipped the thin cotton cloth on her back, she'd stood
absolutely still, giving him one area of quiet in a noisy,
confusing world.

She calmly waited, not touching him, not moving.
Several minutes passed. Solstice's mouth opened and
his moist grip released her. She straightened, standing

a little off to his side. His head turned to her. His eyes, like all horses, set wide so that even when he looked at her, he always seemed to be looking past her. Except this time. She stared at that animal, and he stared back at her without mistake. She saw the white and black of his eyes and within them, a look that seemed to say, ''I was listening.'' Like she had done when she'd first come and had listened and heard too much noise inside him.

THE NEXT DAY she led this animal she loved to the paddock. His trainer had been eyeing the second tier of stakes races for two-year-olds when Solstice's colic had come. His other injuries had dropped him back further. His failure to rally and his willfulness had brought him to today's claiming race. Still he was nickering and pulling like it was Derby Day, and she had to jerk the reins a couple times to stop him from doing his dance. He'd known he was going to race when his hay and water had been removed after breakfast, but she suspected his restlessness also stemmed from her divided attention. Even as they entered the circle of the paddock, she couldn't help scanning the crowd. She was always looking now for Reid and the child. She had hoped they'd be with the Foxes, but it was only Prescott and his grandfather who followed the jockey and Solstice's trainer to the saddling enclosure and into the walking ring.

Then she saw them—Reid, her son, her son—at the outside fence. Reid was watching the horse. The child's attention was everywhere—to the horses, the milling crowd, the afternoon light, the call of music. She heard, "Riders, up," and the jockey came forward for a leg up. The cup of a hand was all the connection she would have with the dark-eyed, dark-skinned man about to ride Solstice, but she willed a win into that palm.

The racetrack workers usually gathered at the course's backstretch to watch the races. Dani, however, headed to the grandstand fence, close to her horse, close to her son and his father.

Another Fox Run groom joined her at the rail as the post parade began. "He'll park," he assured her, folding a slice of pizza in half and taking a large bite. "He's a speedball."

Dani watched Solstice following the pony girl and the palomino. The horse had seemed to relax as soon as the saddle was put on his back. In his gait was a certainty as he went from a walk to a jog to a canter. Even into the starting gate, always a moment of anxiety, Solstice strode in and waited as if already assured a win.

Dani waited, the sun on her shoulders, her hands holding on to the cool metal fence. The trumpet blast sounded. For a beat, the world went still. Then the gates opened.

"And they're off," she whispered, the breeze catching her words and carrying them up, up above to where women in wide hats sipped champagne, a summer strawberry split on each flute's rim, and her son sat beside his father on spindly bentwood chairs.

The colt broke clean but at the first turn, was six

horses back, two lanes from the rail. Still the steady beat to his stride echoed his earlier assurance of being the only winner in this race. He lengthened his stride, passing until he was in fourth position by the second turn. There he stayed as if waiting. Dani saw the hole between the second and third horse and Solstice slip through it as easily as entering a dream, and her voice joined the swell of the crowd as the horse, her horse, headed down the homestretch, the strong August sun turning his coat purple and the daylight decreasing between him and the leader, a gray with white stockings.

Solstice's proud black head was at the other horse's shoulder, then neck, the jockey coiled low on his back, a passenger now. Three strides to the wire, the heads aligned until Solstice lengthened his neck and stuck his nose in front of the favorite's.

The tote board flashed Photo Finish but Dani was already crying, having no doubt who won and not caring that the other groom was chuckling over her reaction to an ordinary race. Solstice cantered, then turned toward the winner's circle as Dani came to meet him. She smiled at him as the results came up on the board, and they moved into the winner's circle but once again, Solstice's looks went around her as if she were in the way.

They came out of the winner's circle and were heading to the test barn when a man came out and hung the tag on Solstice's bridle. Horses that ran in a claiming race were up for grabs, and Dani knew the tag now swinging against Solstice's profile meant another trainer had claimed him. Still she stopped and stared at the tag as if she'd never seen such a thing before. She heard the assistant trainer swear, but the head trainer was stoic, Prescott and his grandfather indifferent. They still got the purse. But whoever had put down the required amount of cash in the racing secretary's office and dropped the claim slip got the colt. It happened all the time.

She was also going away, Dani reasoned. She too had been claimed. Still the reckless excitement of the win left her as she led the animal toward the spit box. She heard a child's voice and thought she was imagining it. Then she heard Reid's voice answering, "Yes, that black beauty there." She looked and saw Reid and Trey coming toward her and Solstice until she was only conscious of the man, the boy, the animal.

Reid smiled and nodded hello as he came up and stood next to her at the horse's side. Her son stood next to him, holding his father's hand, looking up at the huge animal.

The man ran a knuckle gently along the horse's damp neck. "Ready to come home?" he asked.

Dani looked at Solstice. The animal looked right through her.

Hamilton Hills Farm
Lexington, Kentucky

HAMILTON HILLS had been built high on an emerald plateau as if destined for greatness from the beginning. Reid looked out across the acres of legendary lush grass, the reaching lines of white fence and knew the idyllic scene was an illusion. The farm that had set the standard for achievement in the Thoroughbred industry for half a century had died with his brother.

Still, few could view the vast tranquillity spread out before him and not believe a better tomorrow was coming. Reid was one of them. He looked at the land steadfast in its innocence and simplicity and was glad to be home. He'd brought the horse. And the woman. The woman with the deep silence and the sure hands. Her name was Dani Tate. He didn't need another groom. He barely managed to give the men that were left three square meals, a roof over their heads and an adequate salary. But horses were creatures of habit, and it was more than track superstition that made a trainer reluctant to break up a good horse-groom team. Everyone knew the stories of perfectly healthy horses dropping dead for no reason after being separated from a favorite groom. So when the woman had offered to come to Hamilton Hills with the colt, he'd said yes. In fact, he hadn't even been surprised when she'd asked. She seemed to need the horse as much as the horse needed her. Now Reid needed them both.

He headed toward the barns, passing the small white building with peeling red trim that was the workers' canteen. It should've been closed down, but it seemed like such a small tribute to the workers who had remained, faithful to the ideal that had been Hamilton Hills.

He passed the equine swimming pool, remembering his brother's pleasure when it had been built, back when he had mortgaged all their futures, before the bloodstock market collapsed. The pool was empty except for leaves; the underwater treadmills and Jacuzzis used to treat the racehorses' strains and sprains long gone. The private veterinary hospital was shut down also as were two-thirds of the barns, their residents having been led several years ago through the mist, across the fields to the auction block at Keeneland Racecourse.

He rounded the half-mile training track his father had built years ago when he tired of shipping a hundred yearlings daily to a rental track eight miles away. This year, there were only thirty-two yearlings in the training barn. Yet, last season, there had been only eighteen.

One side of the heavy double-wide door on Barn 4 was rolled back, the smells of sweet clover, oil soap and leather meeting Reid as he entered. Smells that had washed through his dreams since he was a child; smells that were now becoming like home to his own nephew.

Several stalls down from the entrance, Bennie Montano was leveling the dirt floor with a wooden rake, humming softly. He looked up as Reid came in.

"Morning, Bennie."

The man leaned on his rake. "Morning, boss." Dust danced in the sunlight trying to pierce the cool, dim interior.

"Everybody settling in?" Reid referred to the horse and the woman, both who'd arrived in the van yesterday.

The dark-eyed man looked at Reid. "She's a woman."

Reid looked at the man who'd been grooming at Hamilton Hills since Reid was a boy. After Reid's father died, it was Bennie who'd brought Reid to the barn, gave him a shot from the bottle of rye he always kept buried deep in the bran barrel and sat with him until the day was nothing but barn lights and deep blue sky.

"That's true. The groom's a young woman," Reid said in a tone that asked if that would be a problem.

"Personally, it don't matter to me. The women seem to have a way about them with the horses, taking care of them as if they were their own kids. And this one, she's skinny but strong. You can see the way she looks at that horse, she thinks of the animal like family. But..."

Reid frowned, waited for the man to continue.

"This crew is all men, and some of them might not be as *gentlemanly* as me."

"Her father was a racetracker. She told me she was practically born on the backside. I'm sure she's seen the less *gentlemanly* aspects of the shedrow and knows how to take care of herself." Reid's frown deepened.

"Then, there's the other old-timers. They'll be wondering why some spanking new sweet young thing gets the new hope."

Reid scowled at his head groom. "She's been grooming this colt for over two years. I brought her here for the horse."

Bennie eyed the other man. "We don't need no more trouble."

The old man was right. Women were common in

the racing world, but a young, pretty girl in the middle of an all-male crew could cause problems. Reid should've realized that even before Bennie brought it up. If he'd been thinking straighter, he would've told the girl no when she asked to come aboard, but he had wanted her, truth be told. He had wanted her for the horse.

"There'll be no trouble. Should you see signs otherwise, I want to know about it, understand?"

Bennie nodded.

"Is she here?"

"She's down in number 20 with the new hope."

Reid strode to the barn's far end, angry with himself and his own shortsightedness. The girl had come eight hundred miles. He wasn't going to tell her to turn around and leave. He could find her something at Keeneland, but, bottom line, he didn't want her to go. He needed her here. He wanted her here, he realized as he moved through the shadows and sunbeams.

He would keep an eye on her and the men, he decided as he passed too many empty stalls. His crew were good men, but still Bennie was right—they were men, and the new groom was a young, single, attractive woman. Hamilton Hills didn't need any more trouble.

He heard her voice like a lullaby before he reached the stall almost at the end of the wide lane. She spoke too softly for him to hear the words but he knew from the singsong rhythm, she was promising the animal only good things. Past the half-opened stall door, he saw her. She was at the horse's side, speaking into that huge black neck that blocked Reid from her view. The light turned the animal's coat blue and the straw gleamed. He heard a wistful, sad note in the soft song now as he moved toward the stall and wondered what sorrows this young woman had. The horse watched him as he approached, then swung his head and curved his neck around the woman in a horse hug. Not wanting to startle the woman, Reid made his steps heavier.

"Good morning."

He sensed rather than saw her fear. If a filly, she would have been skittish and difficult to manage. The colt also felt her nervousness and swung his head up, shuffled his front feet. The woman had been brought here to keep the horse calm. Bennie was right. He'd made a mistake, but he'd deal with it later. Right now, he wanted to calm the woman—and the horse.

She'd already become aware of her charge's shift in mood and had begun the soft crooning that lulled him. Reid saw the calm come over the animal as if bewitched, and he marveled at this wisp of a woman's power. The horse eyed him.

"So you two made it?"

"Yessir." She kept distance between them.

He shook his head. "I'm Reid, Dani. Just Reid."

She nodded, not looking at him.

"So what does our fella here think of his new home?"

"Clover hay, sweet feed, Kentucky bluegrass." She smiled her gentle smile and patted the horse's cheek. "He'll be happy here."

"What about you?"

She looked at him, her eyes again startled as if unaccustomed to questions about herself. He looked away from her mouth, away from her slightly parted, full lips that struck him as particularly vulnerable. The sense that it was a mistake bringing this woman here became stronger. "You're all situated?"

She nodded, stroking the horse's neck.

"Everything satisfactory?"

"Yessir."

"Reid," he reminded.

"Reid," she dutifully repeated.

Something in that soft utterance stopped him. He looked at the woman for several silent seconds before dismissing the sensation. Still Bennie's dire predictions lingered in his mind.

"You've met some of the crew? You rode down with them, right?"

Her hand stilled on the horse's coat. "Yes."

"And you've met a few more since you got here?"

"Yes." Her long hair was sleeked back across her crown in her customary braid, and as opposed to the horse's dark gleam, it turned fawn in the light. She looked at him, waiting for him to make the point he was bumbling toward. The colt shifted his weight.

"You've probably noticed they're all men?"

She looked confused. "Yes," she answered with a high note of question.

"I don't want you to feel uncomfortable." At the moment, he was the one feeling uncomfortable as the small woman stared at him. He saw her cheeks color, but it wasn't until she spoke, he realized her flush was more from anger than embarrassment.

"I'll take care of your horse, Mr. Hamilton—"

He didn't bother to correct her.

"And I'll take care of myself." Her voice was resolute but low and steady, not wanting to spook the horse.

"Good, but should something occur otherwise between you and the crew, I expect you'll tell me directly."

She paused as if struggling with her answer. Finally she nodded.

He knew she was lying.

She knew he knew.

"We'll turn Solstice out today, give him a little rest after the trip. You can check in the training barn, see if they need any help with the yearlings."

She nodded.

"Have him tacked up for training early tomorrow." He felt her gaze on him as he walked back to the front of the barn. He met Bennie coming out of the barn's office.

"What house is she in?" he asked, referring to the tenant residences scattered around the property.

"The one out past the foaling barn."

Reid looked to the other end of the barn, saw Dani's slight silhouette as she stepped outside the stall. "I want her closer."

Bennie scratched his wiry head. "There are none closer. That's it."

Reid thought a moment, his gaze on the woman

until she disappeared back into the stall. "There's the cabin at the one end of the lower pasture. It can be seen from the main house. I'll have it aired out and cleaned up. Move her in there tomorrow."

Chapter Four

Dani halted at the sweep of rich lawn that led to the main house. It was bigger and grander than she remembered. The back, shaded by ancient oaks, was less impressive than the front with its curving portico and thick, tall columns topped with scrolled crowns. Still anxiety overwhelmed Dani's indignation, and she turned to go back to her new quarters without a fight when she saw Trey round the corner of the back veranda, his grandmother in pursuit.

The child squealed as the older woman caught him and whirled him around and around in a lovely dance. The boy's laughter rose in the air like a perfume, and the pleasure and pain rose inside Dani. The dance stopped. The grandmother and the child were looking at her expectantly. The boy waved, and before Dani realized what she was doing, she took a step toward the child.

"May I help you?" Georgia Hamilton asked. Her arms tightened on the boy.

Dani smiled at her son and was rewarded with a

smile back. She looked at Georgia. "I'm the new groom. I'd like to speak with Mr. Hamilton if he's around."

She smiled again at Trey. He was a beautiful child with hair bleached to wheat and Reid's silvery eyes and a touch of the devil in his smile that Dani knew came from her own father. He'd break hearts all over the Bluegrass one day. And she would watch from afar, pitying the poor girls but unable not to be proud of her son.

"I believe he's going over the books in his office."

Dani tore her gaze away from Trey to see Georgia studying her keenly. The woman's thick, pale gold hair was pulled back from her face and caught in a barrette low on her neck. Her slim-fitting trousers and light knit sweater showed she'd kept the trim figure of her youth. She smiled at Dani.

"Follow me, and we'll see if he can be interrupted. But be forewarned. Reconciling the books always puts him in a foul mood." Carrying the child, Georgia started toward the house. Trey laid his head on his grandmother's shoulder and looked at Dani. Once more, she thought her heart would break from joy and pain.

It wasn't until they reached the wide railed veranda that Dani noticed the house's paint was chipped and peeling in several spots, its color graying. The shutters, too, were weathered. She saw Georgia glance at the exterior, her hand moving up, smoothing back several strands of hair that had come loose during her play with her grandson.

Georgia walked with a brisk step, and Dani found herself almost skipping as she followed the woman and the child inside through sliding glass doors. They passed through a series of rooms until they came to a wide hall that opened onto a foyer where a crystal chandelier three stories up caught the sun. When Dani lowered her gaze, she saw Georgia gently smiling at her.

"It's a monstrosity, isn't it?" Georgia's arm swept out as she started down the opposite hall that flanked the curving staircase. "Such extravagance. It's almost an embarrassment now."

Dani heard the echo of their footsteps, the wistfulness in the woman's voice.

"The top floor and most of the second are closed off. Maria and I keep up with the rest. Have you met Maria? Bennie's wife?" Georgia glanced over her shoulder.

Dani shook her head.

"She's been taking care of the house as long as Bennie's taken care of the Thoroughbreds. I don't know what I'd do without either one. Still I've told Reid over and over we should just put this damn drafty thing on the market and be done with it, but he won't hear of it." Georgia glanced over her shoulder at Dani again and smiled. "He'll deny it to his death, of course, but between you and me, my son's as sentimental as an old woman at the scent of the first dogwood blossoms in the spring."

Dani wasn't sure how to respond to this so she said nothing. Trey watched her from his grandmother's shoulder. They turned left and down another passageway.

"So, you must be the new groom who came from the north with the horse?"

"Yes, ma'am."

"Oh, please." Georgia waved her hand once more. "Call me Georgia. At one time, I might have stood on formality, but fortunately, I've since learned it's a useless affection." She gave Dani a sidelong glance. "And what shall I call you?"

"Dani, ma'am. Dani Tate."

The woman graciously overlooked the "ma'am." "Dani? Did your father wish for a boy?"

Dani smiled. "Perhaps, he did."

"Well, it does have a certain charm, but you're much too lovely for such a masculine name, if you don't mind me saying."

Dani smiled at the woman for whom the term "Southern hospitality" must have been invented. How different she was from other owners and members of the upper class Dani had encountered. Dani's own blood had shunned her. She had never expected different from others with the same wealth and status as her mother's family, and she'd rarely been surprised. Until now. "No, I don't mind you saying."

"Do I hear Kentucky in your voice?"

"I was born not far from here, ma'am." Relief broke within her as they left the subject of her name. She'd already prayed her employee forms requiring her full first name didn't give Reid pause. Many women in the world were named Danielle. No one needed to know she was the only one with the middle name of DeVries. The employee papers had required middle initials only.

Georgia smiled warmly. "A Bluegrass gal like myself."

Dani looked to the woman's well-cut clothes, her hair in its expensive blond shades. She saw the ease and deep confidence of a woman comfortable in a world Dani had only imagined.

"I've been away for a while."

Georgia paused before one of the many dark closed doors. "Welcome home." She smiled, and Dani knew she would never think of this woman without affection. Trey rested his head on the woman's shoulder, content.

Georgia opened the door without knocking, her honey-blond presence sweeping into the room, rivaling the glaze of sunlight from the long, leaded windows. Reid looked up from the desk, scowling.

"What'd I tell you?" Georgia stage-whispered to her grandson. "Oscar the Grouch." She set Trey down onto the thick carpet. "Go give Uncle Oscar a hug."

Trey rounded the desk, his arms outstretched. Reid pulled the boy up into his lap, his expression softening. The child was so loved. Dani watched as Reid bent close, his head aligned with Trey's as he showed the boy how to add two plus two on the calculator. He should know the truth, Dani thought. He should know the child is his son. How long could she keep this secret? From outside the doorway where she lingered, she stared at her son's crown, his hair bleached to the color of bone. As if sensing her study, Trey looked directly into her eyes and smiled. Her heart surged with emotion. Not yet. She couldn't risk losing him yet.

Reid followed his son's gaze to where Dani was standing. The frown returned to his face.

"It's not the colt, is it?"

"No, sir. Solstice is fine."

"Child, come on in," Georgia invited. "Believe me, his bark is worse than his bite. Reid, did you know this gal was Kentucky born and bred?"

The anxiety had left Reid's features but his expression was still dark. "No, Mama, I didn't," he said, easing Trey off his lap and standing. "But as pleasant as this little visit is, I do have work to do. So unless it's an emergency—" He glanced at Dani.

Georgia looked at Dani with a mother's patient smile. "You may not believe it, but once my son was as charming as his mother. That's what they said. If I heard it once, I heard it a hundred times. Of my oldest son, Trey Junior, God rest his soul…" The woman touched her grandson's hair and for a second looked all of her many years.

"Mama…" Reid's voice was gentle now.

Georgia continued as if she hadn't heard him. "They said Trey Junior inherited his father's ambition, but Reid…" She smiled at her son. "They said he'd been blessed with his mother's charm. And there was a time when he actually put it to good use." She winked at Dani. "The ladies would fall faster than stardust on a summer night."

"Mama." Reid gestured to the books spread open across his desk.

Still smiling, Georgia moved toward her son, curved her hand along his cheek. "I just want to know what became of that boy?"

Reid took his mother's hand in his. "He became a man, Mama."

Georgia gave a cluck of disgust as she scooped up Trey. "Well, at least I've got you, baby boy. We'll move on and let Uncle Reid take care of business."

"I'm not a baby," Trey objected.

"No, darling, you're not, but no matter how big you get, you'll always be Grandmamoo Hamilton's baby boy." Georgia stopped, put her hand on Dani's forearm. "Go on in and give him hell, honey. And you make sure you come by the house again and say hello, promise?"

"Yes, ma'am."

Georgia beetled her brow. "One more 'ma'am' and I'll feel the need to sit out on the veranda, counting my memories."

"I mean, yes, Georgia."

"That's better. Say goodbye to Miss Dani, Trey."

"Goodbye, Miss Dani."

Dani couldn't resist a touch of her hand against his arm. His skin was so soft, his arm so small. The night he had been born, she had tried so hard to remember every detail. She now knew memory could never do justice to a miracle. "Goodbye, handsome."

"You hear that, Trey?" Georgia teased as she carried the boy out of the room. "I think Miss Dani is sweet on you."

Dani looked at Reid. The smile left her face. He motioned for her to come in, gestured toward the chairs in front of his wide desk. She stayed standing. So did he. He glanced at the computer screen, pressed a button on the keyboard before raising his gaze back to her.

"Is there a problem?"

"I was moved from the quarters I was given when I got here to new ones. Bennie said you ordered the move."

"Yes, I asked Bennie to move you." He waited for her to continue. His gaze once more dropped to the computer screen as if it controlled him. Each time he glanced down, his expression tensed a little more.

He had changed more than she realized. It hadn't been so evident in Saratoga, but here, in what remained of Hamilton Hills, the haunted look seemed to always hover about his features, and his face looked not only lined but as if it had weathered a thousand blows. Still he was the most handsome man she had ever seen.

"The new accommodations are comfortable, aren't they?"

"Yes, of course, but the other ones were also fine."

He rubbed his brow. "So you're not here to thank me."

"Why was I moved?"

"I don't normally need to explain my decisions."

His expression as well as his words signaled he

didn't like his authority challenged. Oh, he was like her beloved Solstice. He didn't like being reined in. She silently waited.

"I decided you would be more comfortable in the cabin."

"Don't you mean you decided you would be more comfortable if I was in the cabin?"

His smile seemed to surprise him as much as it did her. "The Thoroughbreds have perfected your tact, I see."

"I've spent my life dealing with difficult creatures."

The smile became laughter, and she glimpsed the man that had taken her heart so easily. It was unfair to love so simply. How many times had she told herself it couldn't be? She looked at the man smiling only steps away and she could no longer deny anything. Her attraction was immediate and effortless. She stepped back toward the door.

"You want to return to the other quarters?"

"I don't want to be given special treatment. I told you I can take care of myself."

"You're my responsibility."

"I'm my own responsibility."

"You're an employee here. That makes you my responsibility."

The laughing man was gone. She could almost see the burden carried by his strong shoulders, the sorrow he couldn't shake off.

"There will be no trouble at Hamilton Hills. You'll

stay in the cabin. If the men ask any questions about it, tell them to come and see me.''

She shook her head. ''The men won't ask any questions. They'll make up their own answers. They'll see a young woman given special accommodations.''

''All the other quarters are unsuitable.''

''But you've put me in a part of the personal residence.''

Reid looked at her. ''The cabin is closer to the main house than the outbuildings. That's all. You will be safer there.''

''The assumptions the men will make will be far more dangerous than if you had left me where I was.''

He stared at her. ''You will stay where you are.''

''I can take care of myself.''

There was the slightest flicker of a smile in his features. ''I've no doubt you can, Miss Dani, but I'll be taking care of you while you're at Hamilton Hills.''

''Why don't I just slip on a halter, and you can pull me around by a lead line?''

He had the grace not to widen his smile. ''If you prefer, but I doubt the men will let that pass without a comment or two.'' He let his smile become full. ''Indulge me.''

She opened her mouth, ready to protest further.

His smile turned devastating. ''And if I'm wrong, you can lead me through the stables by a shank line.''

She was never a match for this man. ''Your mother was wrong,'' she told him as she moved toward the door. ''You're still as charming as her.''

She had no right but she was pleased when she heard his laughter follow her out the door.

THE BOOKS and bills had taken the afternoon and more juggling than a three-ring circus. The horses had been given their early evening feed and were readying themselves for bed by the time Reid went to the barns. He found Solstice gazing out his stall window. Beyond the glass was the track's oval.

"Don't worry, boy. You'll be out there tomorrow."

The animal swung its large head toward him. He blew out a breath, his large nostrils flaring and turned back to the window. Reid followed the horse's gaze. Alongside the lower pasture, where the ground began to gently rise, a few of the hands were playing Frisbee football. He couldn't hear their cheers and jests, could only imagine their laughter. He himself used to play in the past. Once his entire life had been a game.

It seemed too late in the day, in the season, for bright sun, but still the world was pure clear light. He saw the girl, Dani, in the center of the game. Her hair had been left free about her shoulders and back. It lifted, swirled, fell with her movements, changing shape, changing colors as she bent, jumped for the catch, rolling, then running toward the goal. There was a select grace about her figure as if she'd repeatedly been put through paces. The distance made her features indistinct, but it didn't matter. He remembered her face painted only by the surrounding light and shadow until, at times, she seemed to blend with all around her. Other times, her countenance's natural alignment and richness of shades created her fiercely distinct, singularly beautiful. Times such as today when her clear green eyes had deepened to rich emerald and her mouth had became fuller and more mobile as her words had become stronger.

Solstice moved away from the window, came to the stall door. Lost in thought, Reid looked at the animal and saw Aztec Treasure, white-eyed, white-lathered. Too much white. All that red. He felt the whisper of Solstice's lips against his hand gripping the door. He stepped back as if slapped, looked at Solstice but saw the Treasure...and his brother's still body.

He left the shadows of the barn and went into the day's cool caress, looking to the roll of the land, the line of the sky for peace. But the fear stayed in his blood, hot as the horse's breath had been against his knuckles.

He moved toward the house, to supper and light conversation, a child's questions, a calm he'd begun to cherish.

He'd been confident in Saratoga, but now that the horse and the woman were here, he'd had nothing but doubts. Had it been a mistake to bring them here?

He focused on the white house, its exterior gleaming only from a distance. He tried not to think or remember. The football game was still going strong. Even though he'd deliberately circled away from it, he could easily hear the yells and teasing. Then there was a laugh—a rich, full, feminine laugh. He stopped. His head swiveled toward the pasture. Surely he'd imagined it? The laugh came again as real as his own breath. It belonged to the woman here now; it belonged to the woman here one night five years ago.

He must be mistaken. He waited. The laughter—disembodied yet so familiar—didn't come again. He rubbed his face with his hands, no longer sure what had been real, what had been imagined. The books and the bills had tired him, letting the memories come too easily. The horse. The woman. Hadn't he learned less than an hour ago when going over her forms that the woman's full first name was Danielle? Sheer coincidence, of course. The laughter he heard inside him became his own, mocking him.

He ran a hand across his face once more, weary, thinking of a whiskey. What had he hoped to prove by buying the colt, bringing him and the woman here? From the first, he had looked at them and seen another, remembered too much—a night, a need, he lying content in a woman's arms while his brother lay bleeding to death. So many nights he dreamed of his brother; just as many nights he dreamed of the woman. And as horrible as the dreams of his brother were, the dreams of the woman were that sweet.

He moved toward the house and the respite that would come from food, drink, his mother's smile, a child's laughter. The horse and the groom were here now. His obsession had been born long before their arrival.

He had his supper in the circle of his mother and Trey, their voices, old and young, blending, soothing. Yet his unease didn't abate. He had his whiskey. He poured another and moved to the veranda to wait for the cool light of the moon. The grass was a darker green. The shortening of each day had become less subtle. The song of the night was quieter. All around him the end of summer came.

He heard steps. His mother settled in the chair beside him.

"Is Trey asleep?"

"God willing." She smiled, looking out to the land as she sipped coffee from a china cup. Her smiles hadn't always come so easily, but then a grandchild had come like a gift from above, making even Reid believe miracles do happen.

Georgia set her coffee on the small table at her elbow. She rested her head against the chair and closed her eyes. Age had refined her beauty; tragedy had dramatized it, taking away softness and darkening the silver of her eyes. But in repose, her eyes closed, her lips too loosely parted, she merely looked old.

Reid looked away. "We should interview for a nanny."

"No."

He looked back. Her eyes hadn't opened. "You're exhausted," he told her.

She opened her eyes and regarded him. "So are you." She patted his hand on the chair arm, smiled a mother's smile. She had loved her sons with a quiet, constant joy. Once Trey had come, she had begun to make peace with her oldest son's death. Reid knew she wished him to do the same.

"You work too much," he said.

"So do you." Her hand stayed on his.

He smiled as he sipped his whiskey, looked out to the night falling fast now. "There was a time when that wouldn't have been a complaint."

"It has always been the extremes for you." His mother's voice wasn't judgmental, only factual. "Even when you were a boy Trey's age, it was either complete rapture or desperate despair. Black and white. All or nothing. There were never any grays in your world."

He was silent.

"You are like your father in that respect." Georgia patted his hand once more before reaching for her coffee. "You should marry, Reid."

It wasn't the first time she'd told him; it would be far from the last.

"Fall in love with a wonderful woman, have children of your own, cousins for Trey. The house is too big, too quiet. It was built for family."

"I will," he always said to appease her. Yet he knew she was right. The farm was far from its past success, but slowly, each season, it was climbing upward from the brink of bankruptcy. Hope had been brought, healing had begun when the child had come to Hamilton Hills. Yet Reid knew the restoration of the farm, the family would never be complete until he himself brought a bride, babies to the Hills, letting the future rather than the past reign these lands.

"Cicely Fox will be coming down for the Keeneland meet. She seemed terribly taken with you in Saratoga."

He gave his mother a sidelong glance. "I doubt I

was no more than a curiosity to break up another summer season at the Spa.''

''You underestimate yourself.''

''No, I just don't underestimate Ms. Fox.''

His mother couldn't suppress a smile as she raised the china cup to her lips. ''She was a perky little thing, wasn't she? High maintenance, I imagine, too. She made me nervous the way she was always flitting about.''

Reid smiled. ''The girl did flutter.''

''And that way she'd say 'y'all.' The child came from Connecticut, for gosh sakes.''

Reid chuckled. ''You'll just have to try again next season, I suppose.''

His mother looked incredulous. ''Me? I had nothing to do with that. It was you and your devastating charm alone that drew Cicely.''

''I'm not discounting that factor.'' Reid's smile turned teasing. ''But you also must remember your young partner in crime isn't quite as skilled in the art of discretion as you are.''

Georgia set down her coffee cup. ''What did Trey tell you?''

''That Grandmamoo had told him to be her best angel boy whenever 'Celery' was around.'' Reid smiled. ''I suspect that was right before he tore off across the backside.''

His mother smiled defeat. ''Of course. When else?'' She shook her head. '''Silly Celery.' That's what he called her, you know.''

''The boy is wise beyond his years.'' Reid sipped

the last of his whiskey. He saw a light come on in the cabin and was surprised. Then he remembered the groom.

"I only want your happiness, darling," his mother said.

He nodded. He knew. "And I, yours." He stretched. All was night now. "I better get to bed, I suppose. Tomorrow we begin with the new colt."

"The groom is a girl, I see." His mother didn't look at him but to the dim shapes in the darkness surrounding them.

He said nothing. He wasn't going to encourage her.

"She's lovely in her own way, don't you think?" Georgia's gaze now met his.

He stood. "They're all lovely in their own way."

His mother smiled. "She made you laugh this morning. It was wonderful to hear."

He shook his head. "You're grasping now, Mama."

His mother folded her hands and settled them in her lap, her expression content as she gazed out across Hamilton Hills. "I heard you laughing like you used to. It was wonderful."

"Good night, Mama."

"I was no more than a hot walker myself when I met your father, you know. Your grandmother did everything in her power to keep us apart." Georgia's expression changed as she watched the night. "She almost succeeded, too. God, the woman despised me until the day she died."

She shifted her gaze to her son, turning away from the night's silhouette and her own memories. She reached out her hand, received her son's kiss on her cheek. "Good night, darling. Sweet dreams."

Reid went inside, readied for bed. Before climbing beneath the covers, he looked out one last time across the farm as he'd done since he was a boy.

The light in the cabin was still on. For the first time in five years.

Chapter Five

Dani didn't wait until dawn to go to the barn. She crept in at two. The barn cats warily watched her. She climbed to the hayloft above the sleeping horses and, propping herself against a bale, she tucked her chin to her chest and hoped for an hour's sleep. Sleep wouldn't come in the cabin. She'd lain on the couch with the heavy wood frame until the irony of her chosen quarters and the assault of her own memories had sent her to the stables in the middle of the night.

She half dozed, her sleep like twilight. About an hour before dawn, she climbed down the loft ladder, crept out of the barn and went back to the cabin before anyone caught her. She washed her face, brushed her teeth, and removed the hay clinging to the calves of her jeans. Bennie was already removing wraps when she went back to the barn.

"Morning," he said, unrolling a long strip of flannel from around a bay's foreleg. He cocked his head toward the far end of the barn. "Your darling is pawing a hole in his hay."

She looked down the wide aisle, heard the sounds of Solstice circling in his narrow stall, then saw his proud profile as he hung his head out, his chest pressing against the door.

Bennie smiled. "He's ready to run, huh?"

"Always ready to run," Dani said, moving down the aisle. At the sound of her voice, Solstice swung his head and whinnied a loud, single greeting.

She had him bridled and saddled and was hand walking him when Reid arrived. He nodded to her, his eyes on the horse. Behind Reid, Dani saw Smiley and Bennie's nephew, Angel, heading over from the training track.

"Let's go," Reid said.

Dani led Solstice out and toward the men. Reid walked beside her in the new morning. They had almost met Smiley and Angel when Solstice locked his legs and stopped dead.

Dani glanced at the colt once, saw the sun lighting his blackness. She turned, looked straight ahead to the blue-green hills and stood perfectly still, the reins loose in her hands. She'd played this game before. A few seconds indulging the colt, then a sharp tug on the reins and they would continue, both beast and man satisfied. From the side, she saw Solstice roll an eye at Reid. She tightened her grip, about to jerk the reins when the animal swung his head, hunched his spine and kicked his back legs out. His front legs raised up; legs flew backward, forward, hooves flailing, head rearing. A squeal sounded from the center of the animal's strong, heaving chest.

Smiley and Angel halted at the first buck. Reid reached out to grab the reins but Dani pushed his hand away. He came toward her and the horse until she gave him a sudden shove that sent him stumbling backward. Her hand stayed raised, warning him. He glared at her but didn't move. Dani's hand dropped. She stood solid, impassive, the reins firm in her hand. She didn't look at the crazed horse kicking up a storm only a few feet to her side nor did she look at the men standing in a semicircle, watching. Motionless, she stared out at the track as if daydreaming of a Breeder's Cup win. She waited. Finally the hump in Solstice's back relaxed until the colt stood on four quivering legs. Only then did the groom move, turning to the animal's head and laying her palm to his wide neck.

She glanced at the men and their tight-lipped expressions. "He's just trying to make me look good." She smiled, hoping to ease the worried looks around her.

Reid stared at the horse and the woman, his expression dark.

She stroked the colt around the eyes, brushed his forelock to the side. "You should've seen him when he used to really act up." She kept smiling.

Angel, looking uncertain, took a step toward Solstice.

Reid raised his hand, stopping him. "That horse ever hurt anyone seriously?"

Dani looked at him and knew he thought of his brother. "No."

"That's what the trainer said when I asked him. Now I'm asking you."

She looked into the silver mirrors of his eyes. "Before I came, he'd tried the usual antics—kicked his groom a few times, grabbed one of the stable boys by the shirt, tried to take a piece out of him. Everyone was real careful around him. Real careful."

"And they gave him to you to groom?" She heard the disapproval in Reid's tone.

"Not at first. I used to watch him. I saw how no one ever stroked him, petted him, gave him carrots or treats. His groom was scared of him, did his job as quickly and carefully as possible and got out of there. Solstice was left alone." She looked at the colt, her hand always on him. "But it wasn't unquiet around him. He could smell the fear, the dislike. He didn't understand it, just as those around him didn't understand him. But he could feel it. He was as frightened as everyone else."

She looked at Reid. "He never offered himself to anyone back then, and no one went near him unless they had to. Everybody left him alone."

"Except for you?"

She heard the question beneath Reid's question. *Why?* How could she explain that by the time she'd come to the colt, she had hoped for nothing, wanted nothing? She had lost her child, her dreams, her desires, her expectations. She had come, complete stillness without judgment or anticipation—a silence so different from the cold, anxious quiet the animal had known until then. And so, she had brought calm to the colt.

"Except for me. Soon after I asked to be his groom." She turned to Solstice. "We've been together ever since."

She looked at the sheen of sweat on the animal's dark coat. She'd found her child, and the stillness was shattering.

"You weren't afraid of him?"

"He was just alone." She pressed her hand to the hard-beating pulse in the horse's neck. Alone as she had been.

"He was lucky you found him."

She looked at Reid. If only one day, he could understand.

"Thank you."

Reid looked at Smiley who had been a trainer long enough to look away and let the owner make the decision. Reid looked at Angel. Finally he nodded.

Unsmiling, Angel moved toward the animal. Dani gave him a leg up. Solstice looked to the distant oval. Dani started to walk the horse and rider toward the track but Smiley reached for the reins. "Nice handling," he told her, his face remaining characteristically solemn. He glanced over his shoulder at Reid as he led the horse away. "You coming?"

"I'll be along in a minute."

The trainer looked up at Angel as they moved toward the track. "Slow and steady. Forget about even breezing today. This colt has already had enough of a workout for one day."

Dani watched the horse, his hooves high, his steps light as he pranced toward the oval. She glanced at Reid. "He loves to run. That's been his biggest problem in the past—he fires out of the chute like a cannonball, then burns himself out before the end of the race. But when he paces himself like he did that last race, he comes in the money every time."

"How many times is that?"

She shifted her gaze away from him, watched the horse and rider. Reid knew the animal's record.

"They tried working him a few furlongs with some of the other racers, making him stay even so he gets used to holding back, saving himself. He caused a little trouble though with the other runners." She looked at Reid. "He's not mean, just bossy."

"Like his number one fan?"

Their gazes linked. His tone had been neither angry nor amused.

"Sorry about the shove," she told him. She knew before the day was done, the story would make the rounds as sure as she knew talking soothingly to Solstice before would have only accelerated the situation, even been mistaken for approval. She also knew the story would be embellished with each telling until by the day's end, she wouldn't be surprised to hear she'd single-handedly saved the three men's lives.

Reid waved away her apology, glanced toward the horse trotting onto the track. "Luckily, you were right." He watched the horse.

"Well…" She shifted her weight. "If there's nothing else?"

He shook his head, dismissing her. She turned and started back to the barn when she heard, "Dani?"

She looked back over her shoulder.

"Nice job."

She nodded and moved toward the barn before he could see her smile.

Reid watched her retreat, the morning sun stretching her slender shadow even thinner. How did such a tiny woman wield so much power? The animal had reared; the woman had waited. He'd stood only a few steps away and seen the horse rise, felt its passion and power and unpredictability. Yet the slim woman had stood still, unafraid. As if she understood, as if she too had once known what it was like to act in a fever, lose control, lose everything.

Dani disappeared inside the stables while Reid remembered another animal, another woman, a night that did not end.

What had he done? For five years, he'd been so careful. Now he'd gone out and deliberately brought the danger—and the desire—home to Hamilton Hills.

He turned toward the track. Angel was standing straight up in the irons, pulled out of the saddle as Solstice flew around the oval like a runaway.

DANI WAS RIGHT. By the time Georgia heard the story, the trio of men might have been in mortal peril that morning. Knowing much of the tale was exaggeration and that no one had been hurt, Georgia had smiled, liking the woman who could make her son laugh, yet wasn't afraid to give him a good shove if need be.

"I heard you had some excitement this morning."

"No one was hurt," Reid said, not looking up from his supper plate.

"No, I understand the primary danger was only to a renowned derriere."

Reid raised his gaze to his mother's smiling face. "I was pushed, okay? One tiny shove, that's it. At no time was anyone or anything, including my allegedly renowned derriere, in dire trouble."

His mother patted the corners of her smiling lips. "Not even your renowned pride perhaps? It was the new groom who pushed you, wasn't it?"

Reid's voice took on a patient tone. "Yes, that's correct. The new groom shoved me and, as you and everyone else already knows, saved the day."

He watched his mother's smile widen. "I like this woman."

"I'm glad, Mama."

"What do you think of her?"

"She's a good groom."

That's a start his mother was thinking. Reid could tell by the light in her eyes. "Trey, what kind of excitement did you have today?" He changed the subject.

To Reid's relief, Georgia's gaze shifted to her grandson. "Trey, you have to eat your vegetables," she urged.

"I ate my trees."

"That's broccoli, honey. And over half of them are still on your plate."

"I only like the hairy parts."

Reid tried to hide his smile. "Trey, eat a good dinner, and after, we'll go down to the barns and make sure the horses did the same."

The boy studied his beheaded broccoli, then eyed each adult. "All of it?"

"Three-quarters," Georgia compromised.

"Half," Trey negotiated.

"And all your milk," Georgia said firmly.

Trey looked over at Reid. Reid winked, urging him to take the deal. Trey picked up his fork and heaving a dramatic sigh, speared a piece of broccoli. And Reid's world was simple once again.

DANI SAW THEM FIRST, father and son in the barn's wide opening, backlit by the setting sun. She watched, listening to their voices as they started down the aisle. Trey spotted her sitting at the other end of the barn on an overturned poultice bucket, cleaning a bridle.

"Miss Dani," he called.

She saw his small figure come toward her, no taller than the old, three-legged collie who rose and headed with a crooked gait toward the child. Still, Dani thought she might be imagining it—the sound of her name in her son's voice, the quick, light song of his steps. She was grateful for the barn's gloom, hiding her features while she struggled to get her emotions under control.

"Hello, handsome." She looked into his eyes and knew heaven was made of silver stars. "Who's your buddy?"

He patted the collie's swayed spine. "Bojangles."

She saw the boy's long, thin fingers. They were her fingers. Trey looked above her head, his smile dissolving. Dani looked over her shoulder and saw Solstice's huge head hanging over his stall door, looking even bigger and blacker from a small boy's height.

She stood, staying to the horse's near side, curved her hand around his muzzle and let him nibble. "This is my buddy, Solstice."

Trey studied the horse. The horse studied the boy.

"Would you like to say hello?" She reached to lift him up, but then realized she didn't have the right and stopped. She looked at Reid standing at the next stall. He glanced at the horse with concern but then nodded.

She bent down and picked up the child, his soft, warm weight in her arms. He was small and strong, and he smelled of autumn's air. He reached out, tentatively touched Solstice on the neck, then offered the horse his hand as Dani instructed, giggling as Solstice tickled his palm.

"Like the feel of his whiskers, do you? Without those, you know, he'd never find the fairies and elves all around."

The child looked at her, then at the dust motes dancing in the barn's filmy light. "Fairies?"

"Their wings shoo away the flies from the spots the horses can't reach."

The child eyed the colt. "Was that one?" He pointed as a fly flew from Solstice's back.

"Could be." She lowered her voice as if sharing a secret. "All you have to do is believe in them, and they'll be there."

"Magic?" the child whispered back.

Dani looked at her son in her arms. "Magic."

Trey studied Solstice again. "Shall we give him a bedtime snack?" Dani suggested.

Trey nodded. She couldn't set him down yet. She carried him across the barn, his comforting solidness propped on her hip, his smell new and sweet. She set him down at the feed bin, took off her baseball cap, letting her hair fall to her waist. She gave the cap to Trey to dip into the oats. Then together they walked back to Solstice, Trey reverently carrying the cap in two hands.

Trey gave the animal his treat, laughing as the horse greedily mouthed the feed. She glanced at Reid. He was smiling, watching the boy. Dani looked away, guilt tempering her happiness.

"Okay, Trey," Reid said as the horse gobbled the rest of the feed, "we'd better get back to the house. Your grandmother will be waiting to give you a bath. So let's walk Miss Dani home like proper gentlemen."

"Oh, that's not necessary," Dani automatically protested.

"Actually you'll be doing me the favor," Reid persuaded. "My mother already accuses me of working the crew too hard. She won't be happy if she thought I left you here, cleaning tack after already putting in a full day." Reid picked up the tack and cleaning cloth.

Still Dani opened her mouth to refuse when she felt her son's slim fingers slip into her hand. She squeezed the hand so tiny in her own. "Okay," she relented.

She walked hand in hand with her son down the length of the barn and into the orange night. Once outside, he spied a barn cat and took off to catch it. Dani was left alone with Reid. Together they watched Trey chase the cat. The child's laughter came to Dani in the breeze.

She glanced at Reid as he watched the boy. "He's a wonderful little guy."

"He's energetic, I'll give him that." She saw the soft emotion in his silver eyes.

"And loved."

Reid's gaze turned to her.

She averted her eyes. "Your mother and you—it's obvious the child is loved deeply. He's very lucky." The cat had bolted. Trey was spinning in a wide circle, arms outstretched.

Reid shook his head. "We're the lucky ones—my mother and I." He glanced at Dani. She couldn't help but smile up at him, more grateful than he'd ever know. She saw some release in the achingly familiar face before he turned back to his son.

"Trey," he called. "Come say good-night to Miss Dani."

Dani stared at the man's profile, saw the pleasure the boy brought him. He should know, she thought. He should be told Trey is his son.

"Good night, Miss Dani."

She looked from Reid to the child before her. His long-fingered hand stretched out to offer her a flowering weed that grew along the fence. She squatted down, a thickness in her throat that took her voice.

She accepted the plant, more precious than any gift she'd ever received, and croaked out a 'thank you.' She pressed her cheek to the boy's and felt her defenses crumple. She stayed a second too long, her skin pressed to his, her eyes squeezed tight, her heart praying for control.

She sat back on her haunches. Her hand touched the child's cheek. She straightened and stood, saw Reid's study, worried that her eyes were overbright, her emotions too open. She brushed a hand over her face, pushed back the hair from her forehead, composed her features.

Reid touched her arm as gently as she had touched her child. His gaze didn't leave her.

"Good night," she said, even then not wanting either of them to go.

"Good night." He turned, his other hand in Trey's as they walked away.

"THAT WAS very nice of you to give Miss Dani that flower," he said to the boy as they headed toward the house.

"I like her."

Reid looked at the smiling child. Trey knew Georgia and Reid loved him, but Reid had seen the boy studying the young mothers of his preschool classmates. He suspected the curiosity and wistful longing he'd occasionally seen on the boy's tender features was responsible for the quick affinity between Trey and Dani.

Perhaps Georgia was right. Maybe it was time Reid

seriously contemplated marriage. He sighed, drawing the child's gaze to him. He looked down at the little boy beside him without a father, without a mother. He had been almost a teen when he'd lost his own father, and still, without warning, the pain would rise fresh and crippling as the day his father had died.

He squeezed Trey's hand. "I bet Miss Dani is putting her flower in water right now so she can sit and admire it. And every time she looks at it, I bet she thinks of you."

Trey looked up at Reid from beneath his lashes. "She gave me a kiss."

"You made her happy."

Trey skipped a few steps, swung their linked hands. "She looked happy."

Reid didn't doubt she'd been happy. After all, a child had saved his own shattered family. A child could just as effortlessly touch the heart of a near stranger.

"Miss Dani's nice," Trey said.

"Yes, she is. And so are you for making her smile," Reid added, remembering the glimpse of anguish in those green eyes that had made him look a moment more and wonder what was its source? Yet he knew of no lives that went unscathed. All had their wounds. His hand held on to Trey's.

As they neared the house, he saw his mother sitting on the back veranda with Otto Powers. Otto and his mother had been friends since childhood, and perhaps, Reid suspected, for a brief time, lovers, although neither would ever confess. They'd both grown up poor in the shadows of the moneyed manors. Now both lived in one, although Otto always teased that he'd earned his money while Reid's mother had married hers. Age and success had given the man a thick paunch, heavy jowls and a sure step, but unlike Reid's mother, Otto never seemed to have found peace with the world or himself. His discontent seemed to increase in direct proportion to his wealth.

"Here come my boys," Georgia said as Reid and Trey climbed the porch steps. "Come say hello to Mr. Powers, Trey."

"Hello." Trey stood to the side of his grand mother's chair, staring at a large brown mole where Otto's forehead peaked and met his receding hairline.

"Hello, Otto. What brings you here? Business or pleasure?" Besides a family friend, Otto had been the family's lawyer for years. He'd also been one of their biggest defenders after the accident and during the ensuing investigation.

"No matter what I come for, it's always a pleasure, son."

Reid laughed. "You don't have to sugar me, Otto. You know you already have my vote." Otto had been the county Republican chairman for years, and there was talk of a legislative position in next year's election.

"We saw Miss Dani," Trey told his grandmother.

She pulled the child up onto her lap. "I know. I saw her walking with you and Uncle Reid as you were coming back from the barns."

"She says there's ghosts in the barn," Trey said, resting against his grandmother.

"Does she now?" Georgia glanced at her son.

"I believe she called them fairies and elves," Reid explained, "whose wings shoo the flies off the horses."

Trey nodded. "I saw one."

"You did?" Georgia was impressed.

"Sure. It's easy. Miss Dani says all you've got to do is believe in them and you see them." Trey snuggled against his grandmother. "I like Miss Dani. She's nice."

"And real pretty, too." Again Georgia looked pointedly at Reid over Trey's head.

Otto looked at Reid, amused. "This Miss Dani sounds like she's really something."

"She's a new groom that just started with us," Reid explained, "but you know Mama. Any female comes within five hundred feet of Hamilton Hills and she hears wedding bells."

Otto reached inside his breast pocket, pulled out two cigars. "Nothing wrong with marriage, boy."

"No, there's not." Reid accepted a cigar. "And you'll note my Southern manners prohibit me from pointing out you yourself are the county's most confirmed bachelor."

"That's true. I never did marry," Otto agreed, "but that doesn't mean I didn't love." He took out a gold lighter and leaned forward to light Reid's cigar. His eyebrows danced. "I loved a lot."

He leaned back and lit his own cigar, took several

puffs. He grinned, the cigar between his teeth. "I may not be much for marriage but, make no mistake, I'm a fool for the loving."

Georgia laid her hand on the man's arm. "Some may say just a fool, Otto."

Otto tipped back his head and laughed. "That they may, Georgie. That they may."

Georgia shook her head but smiled. She glanced down at her grandson, saw his blank stare. "C'mon little one." She stood, cradling the boy in her arms. "Time for a nice bath and snack before bed."

"Miss Dani and I gave her horse a snack," Trey murmured sleepily.

Reid stood, reached for Trey. "Give him to me before you slip a disk again."

"Shush." Georgia headed toward the house, the boy tight to her chest. "I can still carry a child in my arms as well as I used to carry you. You sit out here and smoke that stinking cigar and let Otto tell you why you should be spending more time with two-legged fillies than four-legged."

Georgia marched inside the house, leaving Reid standing. He looked at Otto who puffed on his cigar, chuckling. "She'll never change," he told Reid. "Scrappy. She's been that way since we were kids. Once when we were mucking out the stalls, I got her so mad, she stuck me with the pitchfork. I've still got the scar." He stood to undo his belt. "Did I ever show you?"

Reid chuckled as he held up his hand. "No, but there's no need to drop your drawers. I believe you."

Otto sat down. "Your mama was the only piece of sunshine in that stinking backside."

Georgia and Otto's families had been racetrackers—a fact Georgia had embraced, but Otto had only tried to deny. He was probably the only man in Bluegrass country that hadn't set foot on a racetrack for his entire adult life.

"How is she?" he asked Reid.

"She's fine, but still I worry about her. She gets tired, and regardless of what she says, she's no spring chicken anymore."

"She's made of strong stuff, your mama."

Reid nodded, puffed on the cigar. "I know."

Otto leaned back in his chair, observed the other man. "So how was Saratoga? I heard you stole Miss Cicely Fox's heart?"

Reid rolled his eyes. "Mama?"

Otto smiled. "Harmon Fox owns one of the premiere operations in the Northeast. Heard he's thinking of moving further south for the climate."

Reid exhaled, eyed the man. "What are you saying, Otto?"

"I'm sure his granddaughter is easy on the eyes, too."

"You can judge for yourself. She'll be here next month for the Keeneland meet."

Otto removed his cigar, pointed it at Reid. "A pretty girl…an established horse farm looking for a new home…"

"Did Mama put you up to this?"

Otto chuckled. "You could do worse, son."

Reid shook his head. "That's not the way it works. Not for me."

The older man chuckled again. "And I call myself a fool for love? Who would've thought behind that tough exterior beats the heart of a romantic?"

"Only when it comes to horseflesh."

Otto rolled his cigar between his lips, eyeing the other man. "Yes, your mama tells me you got yourself a new horse, too."

"Yessir." Reid saw the disapproval in the other man's eyes. "Took some from the yearling sales, borrowed a bit more earmarked for maintenance, and claimed him. He's had some bad luck, haven't we all, but I know he's a winner."

"Tell me you're going on more than instinct here."

"His sire was Aztec Treasure." Reid didn't wait for the other man's reaction. "The colt could be his twin."

Otto stubbed out his cigar, his gaze hard on Reid. "Let it go, son."

Reid leaned his head back, rested it on the chair. He looked to the new night, watched the cigar smoke lazy drifting, dissolving. Otto had never counseled bankruptcy. Yet Reid knew any other lawyer, ignorant of the Hamilton men's inherited arrogance, would have advised it as the most sensible course of action. Reid had sold three-quarters of the farm instead, refusing the generous loan Otto had offered. Once the insurance money had come in, it'd been enough to keep the creditors at bay, but a year later, Hamilton Hills had still been drowning in debt and Reid's family and the life he'd known falling apart. He'd almost been forced to have Otto draw up the papers. Then Trey had come. And new strength had been found.

Reid looked out to the pastures, the hills' comforting slopes. Hamilton Hills had survived and one day would prosper again. And one day, Reid himself would feel whole again. He looked at the other man. "I can't let it go."

Chapter Six

Reid saw the ghost at two-thirty that morning. Often he woke at that eerie hour. His sleep was rarely unbroken. He'd gotten up, gone to the bathroom. His face, lit only by the moon, looked gray in the gilded mirror over the sink. He went down the dimly lit hall and checked on Trey who was twisted in his sheets. Not wanting to waken him, he'd kissed the air above his forehead, sweet with the child's scent. Reid went back to his room, closed the door, crossed the room and stood in the darkness, looking as he always did to the land.

And he saw her. A white, womanly form following the white fence lines. She stepped away from the boards, moving with a swift grace as if gliding. She turned her head, looked behind her. Her long hair spilled forward. It was the groom. Reid knew it. Yet, as the figure vanished behind a shaggy oak, he touched the windowpane and whispered, ''Danielle,'' wondering if his obsession was becoming madness.

She reappeared, only to disappear into the barn. He

pulled on khakis, still not certain he wasn't dreaming. Still not certain he hadn't been dreaming that night five years ago. Soundlessly, he went down the stairs, calling himself a damn fool. It was only the groom. It was he who was haunted by ghosts that took the night's cover and made a woman into another. Ghosts that let him claim a horse that could destroy him. For the first time in a long while, he prayed. Prayed to forget that night, that woman. Prayed for peace once more. He went out into the night. He looked up at the starless sky as he headed toward the stables and prayed some more.

He slid back the barn door and slipped inside, pausing at the end of the dark, wide aisle as he looked for the woman. He moved slowly down the barn's center, stopping at each stall, seeing only the animals or emptiness. The smells of feed and manure and horses were close and thick, and the sounds of the night's odd hour hushed. But there was no groom. He moved down the lane, wondering if his madness had finally come.

Dani had been settling against a bale when she'd heard the door roll back. From the loft above, she watched him come into the barn and stare into each stall. His chest was bare, his skin marble-smooth beneath the night's color. She looked away. She had no right to stare at him and remember the sweet taste of that skin against her lips, her mouth moving across his shoulder to his neck, over his cheek and chin, feeding hungrily.

She pressed her back to the bale. Memories must stop his sleep, too. Had he seen her moving through the night like a thief? And if so, what would bring worse consequences—to reveal her presence or stay hidden? If she revealed herself, she could tell him she often came to the loft at night, finding comfort in the pungent smells and peaceful breaths of the horses. It wouldn't be a lie, and he, having been born to Hamilton Hills, wouldn't doubt her. She wouldn't tell him it was the hearty cabin with its woven rugs and heavy, masculine furniture, that room, that bed, memories as keen as if the walls could talk that drove her here in the middle of the night. She wouldn't tell him it wasn't only regret that stopped her sleep, but the remembered pleasure, the deep memory of desire that was as much a part of her now as the long-fingered hands twisted before her.

She had to show herself. She shifted her weight to stand as Reid reached Solstice's stall. The horse slept, twitching in his sleep as if remembering the morning's last workout. Reid didn't move on as he'd done before, but stood as still as Dani above him. His hands gripped the stall door, and he stood as if engrossed by the enclosure made narrow by the animal inside it. His head bowed and his shoulders hunched forward, the vulnerable stretch at the back of his neck lengthening, the long relief of his spine rising. There was a moan so low it could only be heard in the undefined hours between midnight and dawn. Dani forgot about her fear, remembering only Reid too was haunted.

She crept down from the loft, crossed the barn, placed a light hand on his still, cool shoulder.

He spun around, ready to strike, and she saw she

should have spoken first. But then the fierce glints in his eyes were gone, leaving only surprise. His clenched fist unfurled, and he came back to her.

"I'd thought I'd imagined you," he said, his voice as vague as this limbo hour.

His features shifted, became sharper. "What are you doing here?"

"I couldn't sleep." She made it simple.

"Neither could I." He looked past her. Even close, he was still painted by the night, his beauty made even greater. He had looked this way when he'd first crossed the dance floor and taken her hand. Dark, seductive, powerful. She looked away as his gaze came to her. "I was looking out the window and saw you going into the barn," he said.

Even with her eyes averted, she knew his stare was too intent, and she worried if the shadows had redefined her features also, making what was plain exotic as she had been that first night. She stepped back. If he interpreted her retreat as guilt, he wouldn't have been wrong.

"I come to the barn when I can't sleep." She tipped her head toward the loft. "I was up there."

He studied her. She was tempted to take another step away but didn't move. She stared at him, waiting. Only if he pressed, she would tell him more.

He looked at her. She wished she knew what he saw. His gaze went past her and still she wished she knew what he saw. But as she'd hoped, he hadn't yet questioned her explanation. He was a horseman and knew a barn could be home. She didn't doubt there had been nights he'd slept in the straw.

As if reading her thoughts, he said, "I used to do the same thing when I was young."

He spoke as if he were ancient. He was thirty. Yet she was only twenty-three and understood. No, the barn couldn't hold the same comfort for him as it once had. Just as she could find no calm in the cabin. He looked around, his gaze lifting to the loft, going to the stalls. She hoped he remembered earlier memories now, good memories.

His gaze found her. She looked away. The world was so quiet and the man too close. Yet even if it wasn't the middle of the night and all around them were dreams; even if he didn't stand half-naked, an image of night before her, she would've felt it. She always felt it, the darkly sexual undercurrent, the rush of need as potent as another night. A night that wouldn't let either of them go.

"There's a foldaway in the office."

She looked at him, her mouth dry.

"It's more comfortable than the bales. You should be able to sleep." There was no suggestion in his eyes. "Come. I'll get it for you."

The gentleness in his voice, the abrupt memory of his mouth made her glance away. He saw her gaze go over his shoulder to Solstice and misunderstood.

"He'll be okay."

She hadn't seen his hand come toward her and she jumped when his fingers touched her forearm lightly as a butterfly landing. He pulled his hand away, rested it on his thigh. Where he had touched her cooled. Her uneasiness didn't waver.

His hand lifted but he didn't touch her this time. "I'm not going to let anything happen to Solstice or any of the other horses in my stables. No matter what they say."

He wouldn't bring up what had happened to Solstice's sire. Nor the oldest Hamilton son. He didn't have to. They both knew she knew the story. Everyone in the Thoroughbred racing world and many beyond knew the tale. It was his burden to have known it first. And remembering his head bowed before Aztec Treasure's son only minutes ago, she knew five years had done little to dim the memory.

"I'm not worried." She looked straight into the silvery light of his eyes. She wished she could offer him more. She smiled. "Solstice is lucky to be here." She paused, added, "I'm lucky to be here, too. Thank you." She was thinking of her son, and the gratitude was too rich in her voice.

Reid's gaze stayed on her. "Is that why you wander at night?" His smile was sharp but not unkind. "Happiness makes you toss and turn?"

She was trying to form an answer, but he raised his hand, palm out, as if stopping her thoughts. "It's none of my business. As long as you're not late in the morning." He put that palm on her arm. She didn't jump this time. "We all have our secrets."

She looked at his strong hand unable not to comfort. She felt the shame of her secrets, her betrayal to this kind man, to their child. She looked away.

He took his hand back as if afraid he was making her uncomfortable, even though it was only the reaching out of one human to another, no more than when a horse whinnies in the wind, hoping to hear an answering echo.

"Should we go get that foldaway?" He glanced around the barn, his expression rueful. "There's plenty of empty rooms available."

She smiled, looked past him to Solstice stretched out, filling his stall. "Look at him sleeping in straw with no more thought than the next feed, the next run. He'd give a good snort if he knew I was here when there was a soft bed with clean sheets waiting." Her smile stayed to hide any other emotion. "I'll go back to the cabin."

He studied her as if not convinced. "Are you sure?"

She nodded.

"I'll walk you then."

She brushed aside his offer. "I know the way. I'm fine, really."

"I know that." He waited until she met his gaze. "Shall we go?"

He took her elbow, and Dani could no longer protest.

They closed up the barn. The moon was still slim and high in the sky as they walked to the cabin but the sweet scent in the cool breeze spoke of daylight and morning. Dani didn't want to be with this man in the silence. Yet she was afraid if she began to chatter the anonymity of the night, the kindness she'd glimpsed in this man would make her bold, make her spill her secrets.

Not yet, she told herself as strongly as the urge to confess had come. She pictured her son, remembered his weight in her arms. Perhaps not ever.

She glanced at Reid's profile undefined in the dark light. He'd had their son for five years. But she'd carried the child in her body for nine months, her blood feeding his blood. She didn't know if she deserved it but she needed more time as desperately as her unborn son had once needed her body to survive. How much more time? Who knew? Fate had given her this chance. It would have to be fate that took it away.

"That colt may be a pain in everyone's backside but he breezed five furlongs in under a minute today. Tomorrow we'll just jog him." Reid's speech was more rapid than she remembered, and she wondered if the silence was unsettling him, too. His cool touch had long left her elbow. As the cabin came into view, he said, "He keeps going like this and he'll be shocking everyone at Keeneland next month."

Dani murmured agreement as she thought how familiar Reid's fragrance had become to her again. The memory of the first time, the last time Reid had brought her to this cabin rose as real as the man too close beside her. They'd been two very different people who'd come that time, almost stumbling in their desire. She glanced again at Reid. They'd been softer somehow back then. They hadn't yet surrendered the sweet beliefs so easy for children. They hadn't begun to search every happiness for deception.

She saw the cabin. She shouldn't have allowed him to walk with her through the night, bring her here. Another woman would have wanted nothing else. She'd been that other woman one night. Now she couldn't afford the clamor of desire. She had to be even more careful than when she picked up her child and cramped her muscles not to hold him too tight, press him closer to her heart.

They came to the cabin. "Thank you for walking me." Dani cut Reid off midsentence, her fear of the man and the night and the memories rising. "Good night." She slipped inside the thick front door before he could reply. She leaned on the door, wondering if he still stood on the other side, bemused by the strange, skittish girl who slept in the straw.

If only she had said goodbye so abruptly on that night five years ago. Instead, she'd said it silently, slowly, again and again, even as his fingers had curled around her face and her body had bent to him like the breeze. She had known it was only for one night. One night. She had wanted it anyway. One night far from rough-hewn walls and dirt harvested floors and the smell of manure heavy in the air. One moment when life as she'd dreamed it became real, and belief was no harder than a simple "yes." She had wanted that night. She pressed her palms to the solid door. She wanted it now.

She moved to the leather sofa, big and proud of its bulk like all the furnishings in the room. She propped her head on the wide roll of a burgundy arm, stretched her legs full length but, even with pointed toes, was unable to reach the sofa's opposite end.

She didn't remember this mammoth couch that first night. She didn't remember any of these smug furnishings sized for people of importance. She remembered nothing but Reid and a sense of everything being in its place—her, him, the way their clothing fell onto the floor. She remembered the moon high and white in the sky, and she being awkward, grateful when he'd cradled her head between his forearms as his weight fell on her, and then, everything becoming as right and perfect as their clothes forming an abstractly beautiful pattern across the floor.

She pushed the back of her head into the sofa's wide arm and closed her eyes. It'd been another woman here that night, one who with a tint there, a shadow here, a drape of silk, had been created to stun. Another woman whose voice had softened at that first revelation in the mirror and had called herself her christened name, Danielle, then taken her middle name, her mother's maiden name, to become Danielle DeVries.

Another woman. Yet that woman lay here now, waiting for sleep she knew would not come.

OVER THE NEXT two weeks, Solstice's training continued—walk day, jog day, gallop day, rest day—in preparation for the Keeneland meet. Sprint times became shorter, swifter. Spirits rose. Even Solstice seemed to have a brightness about him not seen in the dusky August light of Saratoga. He still resisted, but with Dani's soft urging, it was only a few seconds hesitation before he would pick up his feet for the farrier or stand still for the vet. Twice he rubbed his nose on the sleeve of Smiley's shirt, each time, causing the trainer's sober expression to crack. He did pull the screw eye out of the wall once and ducking under the stall guard, bolted for the barn door. However, Dani, who'd run to get some rubbing alcohol, had caught him by the halter and fed him loose hay until he grew calm and took one of her fingers in his mouth in a horse kiss. Otherwise Dani could count on one hand the times the colt pinned his ears or charged his stall.

Dani had two other horses besides Solstice—a roan filly with white socks, big haunches, a throaty nicker and a disposition sweeter than the molasses mixed into the evening feed. Her other charge was also a filly, a bay with less than perfect conformation and also a calm manner as if to compensate for the colt that had come with their new groom. The two fillies often worked out together, but Solstice refused to stay even with any animal and made the others so nervous, he was worked alone.

Dani settled in, too. She did her work well, and, as if to compensate for her colt's unpredictable personality, she was always friendly and helpful to her fellow workers. Any talk about her being given special preference couldn't be proven, and she had learned long ago not to come around the canteen or the barns when the day faded and the muck baskets were filled with ice to chill the beers.

She even stopped creeping to the barn late in the gray-black night. Her bed became the pompous leather chair that buffeted the couch's side. She had angled the chair until she could see the big house out the window. Propping her feet on a matching ottoman, she would sit and stare out the window, thinking, for the first time in five years, she knew where her baby was, knew he was safe and healthy. These thoughts put her to sleep.

She confined her daily contact with Reid to nods hello and informative answers to his questions concerning Solstice. Even still, the encounters left her full of confusion and feeling and fear. It was then she stepped closer to her colt, understanding him at the level where all was electric emotion.

"So this is why you run," she'd whisper and his ears would prick forward, and she almost envied him, knowing running was not an answer for her.

And there was her son. After lunch and before the late afternoon feeding, she'd go to the cabin, clean up and then, sitting on the railed porch, pretending to read, watch. Almost every afternoon Georgia came outside with the child to sit in the Indian summer air and work on her needlepoint while Trey ran in the rich grass. It was a sight Dani knew she'd never get used to, and as she sat on those afternoons watching, wonder filling her, and the smells of life and the cloudless Kentucky sky all around her, Solstice's rare contentment came to her, too.

She was on her way back to the cabin one afternoon when she saw Georgia and Trey already on the green square of the backyard. Georgia waved, motioned for her to come over. Despite her desire, Dani hesitated.

Her respite was never so great that she forgot her fear of being found out. Georgia waved to her once more, so unlike the other Bluegrass gentry who kept their distance and treated the stable crew for what they were—workers who shoveled the dung and sweat as hard as the horses. She saw Georgia's smile beneath the shading brim of her hat. Had the Hamilton family always been so welcome to their stable staff or was this merely a result of their recent losses, reminding them, in the end, all is equal? She couldn't help think what would have happened if she'd come to Reid as soon as she'd found out she was pregnant. She had feared he would have only turned his back on her. Now she knew she'd been wrong not to come to him first. She started toward Georgia and Trey.

"How are you?" Georgia raised her smiling face like a flower, her handsome features encircled within her wide-brimmed hat. Dani gave silent thanks her son had been entrusted to this woman. "I see you often enjoy the afternoon air also."

There was nothing strange about sitting outside each afternoon, reading, yet Dani had to look for suspicion in the woman's smiling face. She found none.

"All too soon we'll be huddled around the fireplace, wishing for spring," Georgia continued.

Trey ran up beside his grandmother. Dani looked at his soft features and lost her breath. She squatted to her knees without planning to and smiled into those silver eyes. "Hi, Trey."

"Hi, Miss Dani."

Oh, that name in that voice. She wanted so much

to touch his cheek, his wheat-colored hair, but she had no right. She reached for the wand in the bubble jar beside the blanket to busy her hands. She blew into the wand's circle and was rewarded with Trey's laughter as magical as the bubbles floating away from them. Off her child went to chase them.

"So, are you happy here at Hamilton Hills?" Georgia's gaze was on her grandson as she spoke to Dani.

Dani looked at her son also. "I'm happy."

"My son says you have a way with the horses."

Dani didn't expect the rush of pleasure that made her head light. "I'm afraid it's more like they have a way with me."

Georgia chuckled. "Bourbon and Thoroughbreds...seems either one or the other is the lifeblood of anyone born in the Bluegrass."

Trey ran up and Dani, still kneeling, dipped the wand and waved it in the breeze.

"He's a beautiful child." She was careful to keep her voice friendly, her comments general as she watched her son jump to catch a bubble. "So goodnatured."

"Yes, he's a blessing." Both women watched the boy moving like air.

"This place killed my husband, then my oldest son. It almost killed me too, until Trey came." Georgia watched the child, but the smile left her face. "I'm still not sure it won't kill my other son."

The older woman relieved the sudden sadness in her features with a chuckle. "Damn September. It always makes me maudlin. But sometimes I don't know what's more dangerous to love—bourbon or Thoroughbreds?''

She tilted her head toward Dani. ''Do you still have family in the area?''

Dani shook her head. ''There's only my dad, and he works the circuit. My mom's people are in South Carolina.''

''And your mom?'' Georgia asked gently.

Dani looked to her son and saw her mother before her. ''She died when I was little.''

''I'm sorry.''

Dani stood. ''I'm sorry for your loss, too.''

Georgia turned her gaze again to the child. ''Oh, this damn maudlin September.''

Trey came running toward them. ''Dani, come here.'' He took her hand and Dani, whose own hands had rubbed and soothed, felt for heat, celebrated coolness, finally, fully understood the miracle of a touch.

''Miss Dani,'' Georgia corrected.

''Dani is fine,'' Dani assured them both. Everything was fine as Trey led her across the yard.

''Look.'' Letting go of her hand, he got down on all fours and pointed. Dani crouched beside him and saw a bubble caught between two blades of lush grass, hanging like a crystal, the reflecting light coloring it a rainbow.

She looked up into her son's eyes mere inches from her own and saw the same shimmery miracle. She smiled, not able to speak.

The breeze blew. The bubble was gone. The surprise was sudden and genuine on Trey's face. He sat back, his surprise mixing with disappointment. Dani reached over and pulling out the blades of grass, placed them between her thumbs, cupped her hands and blew a high whistle. She watched as Trey's expression turned again to wonder. And she knew no matter what happened before and what happened after, it would be worth this moment.

Trey smiled and came closer until something past Dani's shoulder caught his attention. "Uncle Reid," he yelled, scrambling to his feet. Dani rose, brushing off the seat of her pants. She turned and saw Reid with another man standing beside Georgia's chair.

"Were you and Miss Dani hunting for mongoose?" Reid teased as Dani came toward them. Free to do what only she imagined, Reid's fingers feathered through the boy's hair. "Say hello to Mr. Powers, Trey."

Dani saw the other man's gaze on her. "Hello," she said as if Reid's command had been for her. She stopped and didn't go closer to the group.

"Otto, this is Dani Tate," Georgia introduced. "She finally got fed up with the North and came home. Dani, this is Otto Powers, an old family friend."

Otto extended his hand. His expression was smooth, his palms soft. "Born in Kentucky, were you?"

"Yessir."

"Your family must be happy to have you home."

"Actually we're her family now." Georgia smiled warmly at Dani.

Otto turned a puzzled smile to Dani.

"There's only my dad, and he's a racetracker so he moves with the seasons."

"Bet he likes Belmont in the fall," the man guessed.

"Actually this year, he went straight to Florida. Calder Park." Dani shifted, uncomfortable beneath the stranger's gaze. "If you'll excuse me…" She backed away, "I was on my way to the cabin."

"Bye, Dani." Trey said, his hand in Reid's.

She looked at her son. "Bye, honey." She didn't expect the soft tone. She looked up. Otto was still staring at her. She nodded goodbye to him, to the others.

"Dani," Georgia said, "whenever you're in the mood for company, come on over and chat a bit. If you don't see us out here, come on up to the house. We're usually around somewhere. And there's a huge library in case you run out of reading material."

"Thank you. That's very kind of you." She continued to back away.

"Nonsense. You'd be doing me the favor. I love my men." She smiled at the three surrounding her. "But I wouldn't mind a little girl-talk once in a while." She gave Dani a wink.

Dani saw Reid holding Trey, Georgia sitting beside them, three sets of silver eyes smiling at her as if all she had to do was take a step to join them. She turned, headed toward the cabin. Even the two fat farm dogs that ran to greet her couldn't erase the sudden piercing solitariness.

The contentment was gone. She wanted her child.

Chapter Seven

She was grooming the roan filly, lulled by the animal's long warm looks and the rhythm of the brushes when Bennie came to the stall and handed her the cell phone. A call had been transferred from the house. She could take it in the office, if she wanted. She put the phone to her ear as she started toward the room off the barn's entrance.

"Hello?"

"Dani?"

Even through the fuzzy reception, she recognized Mick's voice. Her chest tightened. She was afraid to ask why he was calling.

"Dad? Where are you? Are you still in Florida?"

"That's right, love. Calder. The sun is shining on the ponies' coats, and the garlic garlands are hung over each stall as if it were a holiday. Come join me, Dani. It's horse heaven."

Wherever Mick ended up, he claimed was horse heaven although he and Dani both knew there was no such place. Still he kept searching. Dani had to give him credit for that. Listening to his exuberant voice, she was brave enough to ask, "Is everything okay, Dad?"

"Wonderful." The voice was so hearty. "I want you to join me."

"No." She let the silence play out.

"You shouldn't be there, Dani. You don't belong there." The exuberance was gone, and as Dani suspected, false from the beginning.

"If I don't belong here where do I belong? I'm not leaving." It wasn't her home, but it was her child's, and that was enough. "I spend almost every afternoon with him." Her voice full of pleasure, she took the offensive.

Her father swore. "You're only making it harder on yourself when you leave."

"I'm not leaving. I'm not leaving my son again."

There was more silence on the other end. It was always his silence, what he didn't say, she feared most of all. "Please understand," she begged.

Her father's voice came to her now, resigned and weary. "You're playing with fire. You're going to get hurt. You don't understand."

"No, you don't understand—"

"I do."

"In the beginning, he called me Miss Dani. My son. He takes my hand. Yesterday I read him *Winnie-the-Pooh*. He sat in my lap. He sat in my lap and I read him *Winnie-the-Pooh*." Her voice broke. "You don't understand."

She willed her voice strong again. "I won't leave him."

"The day may come when you'll have no choice."

"I'll take that bet."

"The odds aren't in your favor."

"It was you who taught me to go for the long shot."

"You can't win."

"We all know that—we all know that in the long run, we won't win. When has that ever stopped anybody from taking a chance? This is my chance, Dad. I'm taking it."

There was the scratch of static.

"Is there anything else you wanted?"

"Just think about what you're doing, Dani girl."

She sighed. "I don't think I've done much else since I got here."

"Well, think some more until you start thinking clearly."

"Goodbye, Dad." She hung up. She stopped as she came out of the office and saw Reid talking to Bennie at the barn's other end. Reid glanced her way. She had no choice but to move toward the men, deliberately smiling to conceal any other emotion.

"Good morning," she said, ducking into the filly's stall without waiting for a reply. She picked up a rag to rub the filly and saw Reid standing outside the stall.

"Dani?"

"Yes?" She acknowledged him with a glance, then looked away, started to massage the animal. Still it was there—a physical, elemental awareness that heightened the colors, sounds, shapes all around. She heard her father's words of doom in her head. She concentrated on the filly's coat, the movement of her hands. Reid stepped into the stall, received a nuzzle from the filly, reciprocated with a smooth touch along the line of her elegant neck. Dani moved to the animal's haunches.

"I wanted to ask a favor of you."

She paused and looked at him. The filly swung her pretty head, looked at Reid too as if admiring the man's confident stance, strong features, his long, tanned throat rippling as he swallowed.

"My mother has asked me to accompany her to an affair this evening—a fund-raiser for the county hospital. Bennie's wife, Maria, usually sits for Trey but she woke up not feeling well today. We've never had anyone else look after Trey, but my mother says you spend afternoons with him—"

"You want me to baby-sit?" Dani looked at him, her head losing its shy angle.

"I'll pay you, of course."

She was smiling with too much pleasure but she couldn't will herself to stop.

"My mother says you're wonderful with him."

Her joy increased. "He's easy to be wonderful with. He's a terrific child."

"Yes, he is." Reid was smiling now. "He shouldn't give you any trouble. My mother will make sure he's fed and bathed. You'll really only have to give him a snack, maybe read him a story or two, then tuck him in."

"It'll be no problem."

"You're sure?"

She nodded this time, not trusting the emotion in her voice.

"Around seven-thirty then?"

"I'll be there," she promised.

"All right then. Thank you."

"My pleasure." Reid left and Dani resumed rubbing the filly. "My pleasure," she said again out loud.

THE NIGHT passed quickly, each second so wonderful, that when Reid and Georgia returned home not much past eleven, Dani was still smiling. She answered their questions about the evening, all the time remembering the softness of her child's arms around her neck, the sweet smell of his bedcovers, the touch of his breath as she crept into his darkened room and kneeling before him, watched him sleep. Thank you, thank you, her heart silently told Reid and Georgia while she nodded and answered their questions.

"How was the fund-raiser?" she asked as if they were old friends. She was bold, emblazoned with the warmth of her son's touch on her cheek.

"Very nice," Georgia answered.

"A damn bore," Reid replied at the same time.

Dani laughed, not shy at all. She was daring and lovely, kissed by her son.

"I don't think the young single women there found it a bore." Georgia winked at Dani. "Not once you showed up."

Still feeling heedless from the happiness her son had given her, Dani didn't hesitate to look at Reid. Such an abundance of beauty in one face, one man. Even the dark scowl across his features only served to heighten his countenance's clean lines. Compounding Dani's exhilaration came the low rock of yearning. She could never be with this man. She could never be with her son. These were things she would think about tomorrow. Tonight she would only know she had been with her son. And once she had been with this man.

"I'll walk Dani home and check on the horses." Reid ended his mother's teasing.

Still the twinkle was in Georgia's eyes, and the color high in her cheeks. Tonight in bed, the woman would remember the dances of her youth, Dani thought.

"Maybe I'll have a small something here soon. Nothing like the extravagant nonsense we used to have, but maybe a buffet, some wine and music." Georgia twirled around. "Lots and lots of music." She steadied herself, laid her hand on her son's forearm. "What do you think, Reid?"

Reid patted his mother's hand. "Whatever you want, Mama."

Georgia clapped her hands together. "We'll have a few friends and the staff, of course." She included Dani in her smile. "All the people, new and old, who've become like family to us." She nodded. "Yes, I'll start planning it tomorrow." She took Dani's hands in both of hers. "Thank you again for watching Trey this evening."

"It was a pleasure," Dani said, wishing she could tell this warm, generous woman how truly wonderful

the night had been. "Anytime you need me, just ask.
I'll be happy to do it."

Georgia leaned over and kissed Dani's cheek.
"Thank you, darling."

Dani walked outside with Reid, the lingering
warmth of Georgia's kiss on her cheek and the memory of Trey kissing her in almost the same spot earlier.
Her happiness couldn't be tempered this evening. Just
for tonight, she would let it be whole.

"Yes, thank you," Reid said, not looking at the
woman but to the silhouetted roll of the hills, the dark
peaks of the barns meeting the night. Yet even the land
brought him no peace tonight. He'd spent too much
time today, this evening, thinking of the woman beside
him.

He spent too much time each day thinking of Dani.

And so he had lied to her this morning. It had been
his idea to go to the hospital fund-raiser this evening—
not his mother's. It had been so long since he'd shown
any interest in social occasions, Georgia hadn't even
brought up the invitation and had been wise enough
to conceal her surprise when he did. She'd also been
astute enough not to ask him about the reason behind
his sudden change of heart.

The reason walked beside him now, humming a soft
tune, a shine on her like the starlight above. Because
of her, he'd gotten trussed up and trotted out like a
Thanksgiving turkey, causing the crowd's murmurs to
swell when he stepped into the banquet room tonight.

He glanced at her. She was smiling, humming as if

there was no more perfect happiness than to walk in the silent night beneath a quarter moon.

He looked away. Every day, he thought more and more about her, uncertain whether his attraction was in what she made him remember or what she made him forget. And sometimes, not caring which it was, only knowing he wanted her. From the beginning, he had never looked at her and not seen another woman imprinted on her face and figure. So, he had convinced himself it was her resemblance to the other woman that drew him. But as the days continued and his desire grew, he no longer knew whether it was the woman herself or his obsession gone too far.

There was only one solution, he had decided. The farm was slowly but steadily being rebuilt. He saw how easily Trey took to the young woman. He himself was thirty. It was time he stopped searching for an illusion in every woman he met and found a wife, had children of his own.

So he'd gone to the dinner-dance this evening, and some of the loveliest women in the county had been in his arms. And all he'd seen was the plainly dressed, plainspoken woman beside him who smelled of new hay and fresh air and reminded him more and more of another.

"I guess it's been longer than I realized since my mother has been out."

"And yourself?"

"Not long enough."

Her laughter made him look at her and he saw the unfettered smile that had stayed in his memory since this morning. All evening, women's lips, painted in pink or berry hues, had opened, curved, pouted prettily before him, and still he saw another's smile, a smile that had become so gleeful, so grateful when he'd asked her to baby-sit this morning, he'd wished he'd had something more to offer her. Even as he had sensed there was nothing more she wanted. He didn't know why this woman wouldn't let him go, drove him to pursue other women's arms where still he wasn't free. Nor did he know why she, the opposite of the woman he always remembered, reminded him of that night, that meeting. All he knew was whenever he looked at her, there was a yearning so fierce he feared he would speak it aloud. He looked away from her laughing face to the land.

"Your mother wishes you to marry?"

He looked at her again. She had tipped back her head, turned her face to the moon. He saw that smile, that woman he'd known. He grabbed her arm, turned her toward him. Her smile was gone. He was unsure. The face was Dani's; the desire was the same. He closed his eyes to that face but he didn't move. He wouldn't have moved if he hadn't felt her cool, liquid touch on his cheek. He found her lips without opening his eyes. He didn't want to see anymore. He wanted the respite of darkness, the senselessness of desire. His lips touched hers and he was taken back to that night. He tasted her. Same taste. He was losing his mind. His mouth turned hard and searching as he sank into a sensation that was too much all at once, that promised

chaos and contentment and a sense of coming home—
a home Reid had known only once before.

The confusion was too great; the sensation too overwhelming. The invulnerability he'd cultivated for so
long relinquished too easily. He pulled back even as
his hands still clutched her shoulders.

She looked at him, her lips moist and parted from
his kisses. He didn't know who she was. All he saw
was a woman he wanted, wanted still. He removed his
hands from her. She turned her head, looked up at the
stars.

His hands lifted, but he didn't touch her. "I'm
sorry. I shouldn't—"

She raised her own hand, stopping his apology. She
shook her head but still didn't look at him. "I wanted
it, too."

He reached out, but still didn't touch her. He was
afraid. She was too. "Most wouldn't have been so
honest."

She closed her eyes, hiding any emotion that might
be there. He saw the shudder that took her profile,
imprinted it with pain.

"It won't happen again," he tried to offer.

She opened her eyes, turned her head slowly and
looked at him. She also knew he was lying.

DANI SLEPT in the barn that night. Two days later Solstice tried to buck off Angel. The next day, he nipped
the bay filly. The crew started to avoid him again. The
vet left him to last. Smiley shook his head, counseled
that the colt could be gelded. Yet he and Reid both

knew that was no guarantee and the animal would bring in thousands less if he did have to be sold.

Dani felt responsible. She brought the colt the silent communication, the soft touches that had always calmed him in the past, but she blamed the constant turmoil of her own emotions for the end of the animal's honeymoon behavior. Her feelings swung wildly from the joy of being with her son to the fear it all would end. There was the sound of her father's voice over the phone. There was the constant guilt, the unanswerable question of right and wrong. And at night, there were the memories of desire, the reawakening of need until she woke in a sweat once more.

It was late Saturday afternoon. She worked seven days a week and was grateful. Solstice had been turned out all day but still she heard his restless movements as she came into the barn to dole out the dinner feed. The pawings echoed her own anxieties. She breathed deeply, finding the familiar scents of horses and hay. She paused, closed her eyes, calming herself so she could quiet her horse or, at the very least, not agitate him further. Solstice's rustlings increased.

As soon as she came to the stall, she saw the unnatural sheen of the animal's coat. Solstice was turning in a circle, trying to nip his own flanks. He swung his head toward her as she stepped inside. Too much white was in his eyes, too much wildness in his expression, his movements. She cooed to him as she approached him carefully and gently pressed her palm to his chest. His heart beat rapidly. His flanks were unnaturally swollen. She stepped outside the stall, keeping an eye on the colt. "Get the vet here," she yelled to Bennie.

She stepped back into the stall, touched the animal lightly on the neck. "Now, don't worry," she whispered, a mother soothing her child. "Everything is going to be okay. Everything is going to be okay."

Bennie came to the stall, took one look and swore as he dialed the cell phone. Solstice lay down on his side, his chest heaving, the wide expanse of his flanks bulging. Bennie watched the horse as Dani removed the feed and water. She came back with a thermometer, a stomach tube and a bucket of warm water. Reid arrived and saw Dani kneeling beside the horse's head, patting his cheek, his forehead, his muscled shoulder with a damp sponge. Reid squatted down beside her and the animal.

"You've been through this before with him." It wasn't a question, but a statement delivered in a resigned tone. Dani looked at him. He saw her eyes were as white-rimmed as the colt's. She nodded, patiently sponged the animal's coat. Solstice's legs swung up as he attempted to roll onto his back. Reid stood, pulling Dani up with him. Both narrowly missed getting kicked in the face.

"I want you out of here. It's too dangerous," he told her.

She looked at him. He felt, rather than saw, the same fixed stillness she had used to calm Solstice's tantrum on his first day of training. "No."

Solstice rolled back to his side, his chest heaving. Dani knelt down once more, cooled the animal.

"Shall we walk him, boss?" Bennie asked.

Reid watched the woman and the horse. "We'll leave him like this unless he starts to roll violently."

The vet came shortly and knelt beside Dani. Solstice made a low, hollow sound while Dani gently patted the sponge to his neck and the narrow girth from where the groan had come.

After examining the horse, the doctor confirmed Solstice was suffering from gas colic. He administered a laxative and pain reliever, prescribed five to ten minutes hand walking every hour or so and tender loving care and predicted Solstice should be back to his old self in a few days.

Reid walked the vet out. When he returned, he told Bennie to go enjoy his Saturday night. He'd stay with the colt. Bennie left. Dani stayed, kneeling beside Solstice. His eyes were closed, and his breaths less labored. She smoothed his mane along his neck and said in her low, tender voice, "There now, darling. There now." Reid stood at the stall, feeling as if he'd intruded, and yet unable to look away.

It was several minutes before she looked up, acknowledging him. She smiled but he saw the weariness in her eyes. "He's feeling better," she said.

He nodded. She turned her head back to the animal. Her hand had never stopped stroking him.

"I'll stay with him," he told her. "You can go."

"No."

He knew what her answer would be even before she said it. He watched those surprisingly elegant fingers soothe the huge animal, her fingers cool against the animal's coat. He stepped into the stall, squatted down beside her, caught her hand in his, knowing that coolness now. Those pale green eyes turned to him, washing over him like the water that had cooled his colt.

"I won't let anything happen to him."

"I know that," she said in a voice that told him she believed in him, that she'd believed in him for a long time. "But I can't leave him."

Reid understood. He couldn't leave the animal either. There was no use arguing. "We'll keep each other company then."

"You don't have to stay," she said.

But she knew he did. Those green eyes washing over him. Those cool fingers in his. Beside them, the horse shifted, settled. Reid released her, stood. "I'll call up to the house. One of the men will bring down some supper."

She nodded, her gaze already back on the horse, those long fingers tenderly combing the mane. Her arms were deceptively slender. As they bent, moved, he saw the ropy stretch of muscles, the surprising strength underneath.

Later, after they'd been brought their meal, and they were sitting, eating, the plates on their laps, he said, "You're a good groom, Dani."

She ducked her head as if to hide her expression. The atmosphere had never been easy between them. Now the kiss was always there. He should regret it, kissing her, but he didn't. Still it was always between them now—her taste, the way her eyes had stayed closed a second longer after it had ended, the way he wanted her even now. He set his plate down and got up.

"Thank you." She raised her head, such a grateful sweetness in her expression, he couldn't look away.

He moved to the stall. Solstice had rolled once or twice, gotten to his feet, lay back down. He got back up now, swung his head toward his flanks. "I'll take him for another walk." Reid reached for the line, snapping it on to Solstice's halter.

"I don't mind doing it." Dani set her plate on the floor.

"No. Finish your supper," he said, leading Solstice out of the stall. "I'm all done." He needed to move as much as the horse, a restless yearning within him. It had been such a long time without desire.

He moved out into the cool night, walking, circling, waiting for the coolness to come inside him. He glanced at the horse. "How you doing, boy?"

Solstice rolled a glance at him, eyed him as if asking Reid the same question. The horse looked away, snorted.

"I'll take that to mean you're doing okay."

The horse snorted again, shook his head.

"C'mon now. You should understand. You're a herd animal. It's either flight or fight." He thought of Dani's face, her skin so smooth and clear, he'd almost reached out his hand to cup her cheek, trace her brow. But if he touched her once more, kissed her once more, he didn't know if he could stop so easily this time. He already wanted to go back inside the warm barn and sit next to her in the stillness. He led the horse in an endless circle.

"You know it too, don't you?" Solstice turned a bland stare to him.

"That's why you behave better for her, grow calm, offer yourself. She's the key, isn't she?"

"Uncle Reid."

He heard Trey's voice. The child was running, always running. Reid stopped, lay a soothing hand on Solstice's spine and watched the boy he loved like a son come toward him.

"Don't run. You'll fall and break your neck," Reid's mother yelled, following several feet behind. Trey slowed to a jog. "No farther than the fence."

Trey climbed the fence and hung on to the top rail.

"Did you eat orange mash when you were a boy?"

"Orange mash?" Reid led Solstice closer to the fence.

"It's squishy and orange and looks like horse poop." Trey made a face.

"All right. That's enough description," Georgia said as she reached the fence.

"Grandmamoo said it was one of your favorites when you were little."

Reid looked to his mother for assistance.

"Butternut squash," Georgia explained.

Reid smiled, looked at Trey. "You don't like butternut squash?"

Trey made another face.

"Did you put maple syrup and lots of butter on it and stir it all up?"

"I suggested that," Georgia said. She looked tired. "He said no."

"There you go then." Reid looked at Trey. "You don't want to eat orange mash without maple syrup and butter. Take my word for it."

The boy stared up at him as if Reid had all the answers. That look of complete and utter trust made Reid wish he did. He did know no matter what, he'd never do anything to break the trust he saw right now in this child's face.

Trey looked past him and waved. Reid glanced over his shoulder. Dani was standing at the barn door, watching them. She raised one of the plates she held in each hand in greeting and started toward them.

When she reached them, Trey asked, "Dani, do you like orange mash?"

She smiled a big smile at Trey. "That depends." She glanced at Reid for a clue.

"Butternut squash," he supplied.

"There were no nuts in it," Trey argued. "I know nuts. Peanuts. Hognuts."

"Hognuts?" Georgia looked at him as she took the supper dishes from Dani.

Trey turned to his grandmother. "*Horace Hognuts.* That's what Uncle Reid said when he tripped over my Galactic Sky Explorer last week."

Georgia looked at her son. He smiled, shrugged. "It could have been worse."

"I realize that," she said. "Okay, my little man." She turned to Trey. "Say good-night to your uncle Reid and Miss Dani. You need a bath and a bedtime story. Uncle Reid and Miss Dani have to take care of Solstice. He has a tummy ache."

Leaning over the top rail, Trey reached his arms out. "Good night, Uncle Reid."

Reid handed the lead line to Dani and walked to the fence to give the child a hug and kiss good-night.

"Now you be good," Reid told him. "Don't do anything to make your grandmother say 'Horace Hognuts.'"

Trey giggled and Reid bent and kissed the boy's forehead one more time before he left. Trey looked at Dani.

"Good night, Trey," she said. "Sweet dreams."

The child's small arms reached out again, this time for her.

Reid smiled as he took the line from her. She stared at him.

"He's waiting for his good-night kiss," he whispered as if she might not understand.

But she did understand. She understood this and nothing else as she stepped forward into her son's embrace.

Chapter Eight

Dani and Reid stayed with Solstice all night. They kept the conversation to generalities, the easy talk of horse talk, carefully choosing their words, each watching the other's lips. They took turns napping. When each woke, they knew they had been studied then, too. The hours grew late, then early again. Still the river of awareness did not cease. Several times Reid urged Dani to go to the cabin and sleep, but she refused. She couldn't leave Solstice. She would never leave anything she loved again.

She went out into the night to walk, hoping to escape her own heated flesh until she felt safe enough to sit near the man waiting inside the barn. When she went back in, she saw Reid sitting before a leather game board on a bale, setting disc-shaped pieces in a pattern across it.

He looked up at her. "Backgammon. I found it in the desk in the office." He looked at the board and the rows of circles. "My brother loved this game." It was only the second time she'd ever heard him mention his brother. "Do you play?"

She shook her head.

"It's been years for me too, but it's easy." He indicated the folding chair opposite him.

She sat opposite him. He was staring too intently at the brown and white pieces between them. He raised his gaze, released a sigh, smiled apologetically "God, I'm tired."

"You must miss him very much."

Reid looked at her, then stared again at the board.

"I'm sorry about your brother." She had wanted to tell him as soon as she'd heard it had happened. She had wanted to run to him, hold him. But she had been many miles away and always in a different world than him. She had wanted to tell him for so long, she said it again. "I'm sorry."

Reid's head came up, his eyes focusing as if he'd been a long way off. He didn't answer. Yet, as sure as she'd known Solstice had needed her stillness, Dani knew this man needed sound, words, noise. This man had been silent too long.

"My mother died when I was young. Some say it's harder when you're a small child. Some say it's easier. I don't know." It became hard to be so brave beneath his stare. She looked past him to an empty stall. "There never seems to be a right time to die."

Their gazes found each other. His eyes were a flat gray. She decided to be fearless.

"My father says it's not the now of death that's the worst. He says you're at your strongest then, ranting, grieving, carrying on and feeling all the more powerful still.''

She measured her words to the pulse in Reid's jaw. "It's later, much later, in the quiet moments. You're washing your face, slicing a sandwich, folding a newspaper, when the memory comes as sudden and fresh and unbelievable as at first.''

His expression became nothingness. She spoke to the man beyond that mask.

"It's the quiet, quiet moments, my father says, that will kill us all.''

He got up as if to get away from her. He went to Solstice's stall. The worst of the animal's pain had passed, letting him sleep. Dani looked at the man standing at the stall, his back turned to her. His pain was far from over. She feared he would remain silent, although she had been unable to. No more silence. She was about to speak again when she heard his voice as if it came from a distance.

"Some said the stallion, always too high-strung, had gone crazy, ruined from overbreeding. Others talked about my brother's excessive spending, overselling the stallion's genes, how the horse was worth more dead than alive—especially to a horse farm on the brink of bankruptcy.'' Finally released, the words came rapidly. "None of us had known how fast and deep Hamilton Hills was sinking. My brother was ten years older than me. He'd run the farm since my dad died. I was busy with parties and women.''

Reid stood straight and still, his back braced. His

hands gripped the stall door. Several seconds passed. Still she waited. His silence had been broken.

"The thing is my brother loved that horse. Like you love this one." His shoulders dropped. The weight was becoming too heavy. "He wouldn't have harmed that animal." His hands curled into fists. "And that horse wouldn't have deliberately hurt my brother."

He paused. Dani waited. Everything was stiller than she ever thought possible. There was only Reid's voice.

"No."

One syllable. Grief had never been more eloquent.

She stood, her knee knocking over the game board and the pieces falling, sounding in the silence. She went to him and touched his shoulder. He turned and fell into her arms. He took her offered mouth, parting her lips as if he wanted to split them, his own mouth wide in a soundless roar. His hands were huge as they gripped her head. His tongue pushed into her, his lips pressing the flesh to her teeth. She twisted her mouth and gave him hold, giving freely. There was total lock, a raw, punishing kiss meant to satisfy his anger, his needs. She parted her lips wider. Their tongues touched. She tasted his bitterness, tried to swallow it whole. It was all she could give him now.

No more silence, no more silence. The thought wouldn't release her. Yet if she told him everything now, it'd be over. It was too soon, too sudden. He was too confused, too angry.

She drew his tongue further into her mouth, feeding his passion, securing her silence, feeling a traitor.

She had given her child up once. She wouldn't give him up again.

He drew back, taking great draughts of air, his grief reduced to tremors of breath. He touched her forehead, her temple, her cheek like a blind man, never looking into her eyes. His brow dropped to her collarbone. She ran her palm along his dark crown. His hair spilled on to her shoulder and she touched it with her lips. She groped for his hand, found it, wouldn't let go. The shadows surrounding them lightened. His breathing eased.

This was all she could give him now.

IT TOOK several days for Solstice to recover, but only that one night to change Dani and Reid's relationship. Neither brought it up. They knew things like that could happen in a night, things that couldn't be discussed, that would be dismissed during the day. So silence came again to Reid and Dani.

The Keeneland meet was drawing near. It was the shortest meet in racing, only sixteen days, but in that time, millions could be won. The colic had delayed Solstice's training, but the interruption had seemed to do the colt more good than bad. He returned to the oval even faster, flying over the track, then trotting around with his neck arched, eyes alert as if looking for the winner's circle. The crew began to watch his sessions, and even Smiley, in an uncustomary show of excitement, had slapped his thigh and said, "He'll go to the wire, for sure," after one particularly successful workout.

Reid felt the excitement, too, and one afternoon, before he went to his office to do some ordering, he headed to the kitchen to share Solstice's most recent time with his mother. He found Trey with Dani on the veranda. It was late in the day, but the sun was still strong, and the woman and child sat in its rays at the round table on the back deck, chunks of modeling clay spread out between them. He paused at the sliding glass door, watching them, Trey's slender fingers, Dani's dancing hands that quieted a colt, a man, that now patted a boy's arm.

Reid slid back the door and Dani raised her head. She smiled a small, shy smile of welcome. He felt the need to go near her as necessary as his next breath. Her gaze dropped to Trey as she spoke to the boy. He turned, saw Reid and slid off his chair, coming to him with the wonderful awkward arm-flapping run of a four-year-old. Reid gathered him in his arms and brought him tight to his chest. This child could have been his own son, his love was so strong.

He carried the child to the table and sat next to Dani. Trey, never still for long except when sleeping, slid off his lap. "Look what me and Dani did."

"Dani and I," Reid corrected as he looked over the primitive animal shapes and the beginning of what he assumed was a log cabin. Dani rolled some clay beneath her palm, back and forth across the table, forming a longer and longer, skinnier and skinnier snake.

"I also made a picture for Grandmamoo." The boy started toward the house.

"Trey!" Reid and Dani called at the same time.

They looked at each other. Reid smiled. Dani dropped her gaze to the snake still forming beneath her palm.

Trey turned and looked back.

"Where are you going?" Reid asked.

"To get the picture," Trey told him with a child's exasperation.

"All right. Go ahead." He watched the boy go into the house, looked back at Dani. She concentrated on her clay. He touched her hand, stilling it. He didn't want her to be afraid of him. He was afraid enough for both of them.

He took the thin snake she'd formed, doubled it, broke off a piece, smoothed it with one roll across the table, then added it to the log cabin. He looked at her. She'd been watching him, but now she looked away, at the clay cabin. Still she was smiling.

"Your mother had to run some errands in town. I offered to stay with Trey."

"That was very generous of you."

She glanced at him, looked away again, shook her head. "No."

He studied her profile for a minute, always reminded of another. "So what's harder? A four-year-old boy or a four-year-old Thoroughbred?"

Finally she looked at him, a light in her eyes that hadn't been there before. "Neither." The shine in her eyes confirmed her sincerity.

The sliding glass door opened. Dani gazed at Trey coming out of the house. "He's wonderful. Such a good boy. He's been brought up well."

"To my mother's credit."

"To both your credit." Dani looked at him. "You care for him as if he were your own son." Her eyes were darker now, the color of moss.

He looked at the child coming toward them. "I've never thought of him as anything less. And never will."

Trey laid the picture on the table, smoothing the corner wrinkled from being clenched in his fist. "See, here's the sun. Grandmamoo says it warms our heads and our hearts. And here's the grass. Dani can make it whistle." Trey looked at Reid. "She's teaching me, too." His gaze returned to the picture. "These are flowers and here's our house."

Reid picked up the picture. "It's beautiful, Trey. Your grandmamoo is going to love it as much as she loves you. I bet even right now, she's rushing around, hurrying to get home to her sweet Bo-Bo."

Trey smiled. He looked at Dani, pointed to his chest. "That's me."

Dani smiled back. "That's you."

Reid picked up another chunk of clay, rolled it between his palms. "What are you building here? The Eiffel Tower?"

Trey looked at Dani and rolled his eyes, making the woman laugh. Reid lost himself in the sound for a moment, thinking how easily a child brought happiness to others. He thought of his own recent decision to seriously search for a wife, start a family of his own. The other night he'd even let Otto drag him to some Republican fund-raiser where he'd met many women—all smart, pretty, successful. But truth be told, he was having more fun sitting here in the sun, building a clay cabin with Trey and the woman beside him.

"It's a barn," Trey announced as if it were obvious.

"A barn…what else?" He caught Dani's eye, gave her a wink.

She looked away but the small, shy smile stayed on her face.

Reid placed his clay log on top of the others. He had come home to do some work. He looked at Dani as she softly asked Trey where they should start the barn door. Reid reached for another piece of clay.

Georgia came home to find them building a clay fence for a pasture. Reid looked up and met his mother's eyes. He saw the slow smile curve her lips and realized what a quaint picture the three of them must make. He pushed back his chair.

"Oh, no." Georgia came out onto the porch, reading his mind. "Don't get up. It's almost dinnertime anyway. You might as well wait and do any work that has to be done after that."

Dani set down her clay, brushed her hands off. "Is it that late?"

As she rose, Maria came to the back door. "Trey, if you come in now and wash your hands for supper, you can help me choose a vegetable."

Trey considered. "No orange mash." He looked at Dani as he slid off the chair. "C'mon," he told her resignedly. "We gotta get washed up."

Reid saw the pleasure in Dani's face. He'd often glimpsed an unknown pain on that face. But then there were moments such as this when the woman was only joy. "Thank you, Trey, but your uncle Reid and your grandmother are home now. I've got to go."

"Stay." The invitation was out of Reid's mouth before he'd even realized the request. He wanted her near him. The presence of her body, the sound of her voice. Where all before had seemed vague and unreal, now, in Dani, it had taken shape, solidified. He understood why the colt came to her and quieted. He was beginning to understand why he, with all his constant questions, could look at her now and ask nothing.

"I promise I won't pick orange mash for the vegetable," Trey said.

"Oh, that's very kind of you both—" Her lovely, smiling face looked at each of them.

"Nonsense," Georgia joined in. "Maria always cooks enough for a small army. There's plenty. You'll stay."

"We would be honored if you would join us." Reid made his tone deliberately formal, hoping to sound silly and hide any emotion that could slip out and reveal him. He glanced at the boy for assistance. Trey recognized a game, and giggling, bowed from the waist.

Dani stopped smiling as she looked at them both. Reid saw an emotion he couldn't define flicker across her face. But the light still shone in her clear eyes as she nodded and accepted their invitation.

SHE SAT at the dinner table that evening opposite Trey, Reid at one head of the table, Georgia at the other.

The boy and the man seemed determined to charm their guest and took turns making her soft laughter come. Reid watched Dani butter Trey's roll. He poured the boy a glass of milk and glanced at his mother, thinking how happy she looked as she watched those around her, laughing and talking and sharing a meal.

He looked at Dani as she passed him Trey's reluctant choice of vegetable—green beans. "Thank you," he said, taking the bowl. She nodded, smiling her slight smile as she turned her attention to her plate. He studied her profile. He still saw traces of the woman of five years ago, but it was this woman of flesh and blood beside him now that brought him peace. A peace he'd never known before except once, in another woman's arms. A peace he'd never expected to find again. *Thank you,* he thought but to who he didn't know, feeling ridiculously foolish and out of his element and not minding at all.

Dani knew she had no right to sit here between her child and the boy's father and grandmother as if she belonged, as if she were part of this family. Yet here she was. Happy.

She watched Trey slide the child's plate over to cut his roast beef into smaller pieces as he asked about the boy's day. She listened to the child telling them all about nothing and everything, hopping off and on his chair, caught up in the excitement of his own stories. She heard the grandmother ooh and aah in all the right places and every few minutes, encourage the child to take a bite of his dinner. Dani saw Reid eating, listening to the child's chatter and smiling silently, looking up once to catch Dani's eye and share an adult smile over something the child had said. *This is what it would be like to be a family,* Dani thought. *This is happiness.* She looked down, concentrated on her meal until the thick longing within her passed and she could swallow again.

It was over too soon, such a simple meal that never should have been. Yet it had happened. She had sat with her son and her son's father and grandmother, shared their supper, but now it was done. She insisted on helping clean up and doing the dishes. After much protest, Georgia relented. Reid took Trey with him to the barns.

"Let me just put this coffee on," Georgia said, "and we can have it out on the veranda after we finish. By the end of the month, it'll be dark at this time and becoming too cold to go outside, much less sit on the porch."

Through the window over the sink, Dani saw the slow ascent of colors that proved Georgia's predictions. She saw Reid and Trey walking toward the barns, Trey's hand in his father's. She had never expected to be rational when it came to her son. She knew too well a mother's love is unlike any other, and nothing if not all emotion. Yet she had foolishly thought any feelings for Reid could be controlled.

She gathered more dishes off the island counter. When she came back to the sink, she saw Reid and Trey had reached the barns. They stepped inside and were gone—her child who would never truly be hers and the child's father who had been hers once but never again.

You fool, she thought, furiously wiping a plate. *Love them both and you'll lose them both.*

The dishes were done and the dessert and coffee ready by the time Reid and Trey came back. The air turned too cool after all as soon as the sun had dropped so they had dessert inside. After, Georgia told Trey to give her ten minutes to run his bath, then join her in the upstairs bathroom. Dani picked up the dessert plates and coffee cups with Trey's help while Reid took a telephone call. He came back into the room as they finished cleaning up.

"Good job," he told Trey, lifting the boy in his arms. "I'll bet Grandmamoo reads you an extra story tonight for being such a big help." He winked at Dani over the boy's head. "Now let's get you upstairs for your bath."

"I'll say good-night, too," Dani said, "and be on my way."

"Trey, tell Dani good-night."

"Kiss," Trey said, his head resting on Reid's shoulder. Reid smiled, carried the boy to Dani. Trey raised his head, opened his arms.

"Good night, sweetheart." Dani received the child's kiss, pressing her cheek to his and hugging his narrow shoulders, careful not to touch Reid. She smoothed his hair, kissed his forehead. "Sweet dreams."

Reid looked at her above the boy's head. "Wait a minute. I'll be right down to walk you to the cabin."

"That's not necessary, thank you."

Trey looked at her, his eyes silver coins. "What about the Boogeyman?"

Dani had no argument.

Reid's expression was equally solemn. "Yes, what about the Boogeyman? Wait here and I'll be right down."

Before she could protest further, Reid carried Trey up the stairs. She stood, waiting, renewing her resolve to keep her feelings for Reid in check. He came down the stairs.

"Do you have your Boogeyman Blaster?" she asked.

He smiled, patted his hip pocket. "Never leave home without it." They started toward the back door.

"We'll be sending Solstice to run at Keeneland at the end of the week," he said.

"He'll win," she said.

He smiled. "I wouldn't venture to predict anything about that black beast." Even he heard the affection in his tone. The animal had gotten under his skin. He looked at the woman walking stiffly beside him. The animal and his headstrong groom.

"He'll win," she insisted.

"I want him to have some solid tests before entering any stakes races."

"He'll win."

He stopped, smiled down at her, pleased when she finally turned to him and smiled back. Their gazes locked, held. Reid didn't know, certainly didn't understand what was between them. An attraction, a connection, electricity. He took a half step toward her, stopped when he saw the fear in her eyes.

"Dani?" he questioned her. She twisted her head away from him, her braid swinging forward across her chest but she didn't step back.

He moved toward the door, damning his own desire. He had seen the fear in those green eyes, had made it stronger.

"We lost some time because of the colic, but he's been back in full training for the past week and holding his own. But if you see even the slightest thing wrong, suspect anything, let me or Smiley know immediately." He retreated to the safe talk of horses.

She nodded beside him, kept her gaze forward as they went out onto the veranda.

"You're his key, you know."

She turned her head, her braid still long against her slender neck and her arms folded tight across her body.

"Every horse has a key. Find it and you unlock the mystery, open up the door. You're Solstice's key. He knows it, and so do I."

"I'm his groom, that's all." Yet her arms released, dropped to her sides.

"You're more."

She didn't smile but he saw pleasure fill her features before she looked away. "Thank you." Her voice was hushed. "And thank you for supper."

"Thank you for watching Trey today. I'll adjust your paycheck accordingly." He moved toward the porch steps.

"No charge," she said.

"That's generous, Dani, but—"

"No charge," she insisted.

He looked at her. Her arms folded across her chest again. He knew if he offered once more, he would insult her. "Then there must be something else I can do for you?"

She looked at him, the controlled expression on her face softening with gratitude. "No, there isn't. Except…" He watched her face turn sly. "Let me walk home by myself."

"Trey would never speak to me again if I let the Boogeyman get you."

She moved to the top step. "I'm a big girl, Reid. I can find my way."

He saw the earnest plea in her eyes and relented. He had wanted to make her feel safe, not scared. "I'll stand out here and watch until I see the light on in the cabin."

She gave him an exasperated glance but brooked no argument, knowing it was a miracle he'd relinquished his Southern manners and agreed this far. She started down the steps. "Okay, Mr. Boogeyman, I'm a-coming." She heard his laughter behind her, felt its low call and took two more steps, grateful to reach solid ground.

"Good night, Dani." She heard the amusement still in his voice.

"Good night, Reid." She raised her hand in farewell but didn't risk turning around, seeing his figure, strong and large and masculine, above her. She waited until she reached the cabin, blinked the lights on and off in a mocking signal, then settled in the chair turned toward the window framing the main house. Only then did she search the dark until she found him, an outline against the house lights illuminating the veranda. He stood there for a long time. She sat in the chair for an equal length, watching him from the distance. The distance she had promised herself she would put between herself and this man. Because it wasn't the things outside that went bump in the night that scared her. It was her feelings for this man she feared most of all.

Chapter Nine

At the morning's coldest hour, the Hamilton Hills'
team arrived at the Keeneland Racecourse. Later,
when the sun shone full and the air became like a
courtesan's caress, Solstice would run. In the mean-
time, there was the routine of the racetrack—workouts,
walks, rubs, wrappings. Solstice had been entered in
the fifth race, a one-mile allowance on the dirt with a
purse of fifty-four thousand. He and the other Hills'
horses running today had been transported last night,
and this morning, the colt seemed unusually relaxed,
even in the strange stall. Dani had found him still
prone at sunrise, had smiled as he'd levered himself
up and bringing his head to hers, had looked at her
calmly. Today had come without surprise to Solstice.

"Okay," Dani agreed. "Let's do it."

She listened to the shedrow talk as she did her
chores, hearing who ran the fastest time that morning,
who won the last time out, who was sure to go to the
wire, who was certain to balk coming out of the gate.
She saw Reid and Smiley discussing strategy with the

jockey. Solstice had drawn the third position off the inside rail, and Reid was smiling. He caught her eye, sent her a silver wink before she could avert her gaze. She turned, closing her eyes, letting the sounds of the shedrow swirl around her and saw in the blackness, Solstice, Reid, even herself, in the winner's circle.

Before noon, her chores were done, and there was nothing left to do but wait. She left Solstice content in the white barn and followed the walkways from the backstretch barns to the track. She stopped and bought a hot dog and a soda but was too edgy to eat and, after two bites, chucked her lunch into a trash can.

"That would've done better in your stomach than the trash. You're skin and bones now, girl."

She spun around to the voice behind her, meeting her father's devilish grin—the one her son had inherited. "What are you doing here?"

Mick pushed his flat cap back and eyed his daughter. "That's a fine howdy-do." He opened his arms. "Come here and give us a kiss and hug and all's forgiven."

She stepped into her father's embrace, smelling the familiar scents of horse and Irish whiskey. She kissed his cheek made brown and leathery from a life in the sun. The shoulders she hugged were rounded. The man who held her was diminishing.

She stepped back. He kept her hands in his. She saw the smile that always made her smile. Today was no exception. "Sorry. It's just I'd thought you'd stopped surprising me a long time ago," she told him.

He smiled. "Never happen. Mick Tate always has

a trick or two up his sleeve. You should know that by now, Dani girl.''

Yes, she thought, she should know that by now. ''When did you leave Calder?''

He released her hands. ''Came up a few days ago. Change of scenery to keep things from going stale.'' He looked around, nodding satisfaction. He looked back at his daughter ''Kentucky's always home, isn't it, Dani?''

She looked at him for a quiet second. She'd learned long ago a ''change of scenery'' was merely an euphemism for needing to lay low for a while. ''How deep are you in this time?''

He threw back his head and laughed. Such a rich laugh he'd been given. It made those around him, complete strangers, smile as they passed. Everyone but Dani.

''Darling, your dear ol' Dad has actually been on a roll.'' He removed a gold money clip from inside his breast pocket. It was full with cash. ''And I'm going to bet a third of it on your baby this afternoon in the fifth. How 'bout you?''

''You know I don't bet.''

''Wise woman, my daughter is. But still you're a racetracker. So, you're not above taking risks, are you?''

''What are you talking about?'' she asked although she already knew.

''I've been watching you all morning.'' He studied her. ''You're happy, aren't you?''

She lowered her voice. ''I have my son.''

He shook his head. "No, you don't, honey. He may be nearby but he doesn't belong to you." He met her eyes. "He can never belong to you."

"I'm with him now. That's all that matters."

"What about tomorrow or the day after that? One day the truth will come out. What will happen then? When the Hamilton family and your son—your son, Dani—learn who you really are? Who he really is? What do you think they'll do then? Embrace you with open arms? Invite you to scrape the horse crap off your sneakers and sit at their table?" He snorted. "They'll throw you out faster than last night's straw."

"They won't find out."

Mick took out a pack of cigarettes, tapped one out and lit it, all the time staring at his daughter with narrowed eyes. "Pretty high stakes for a non-betting girl."

Anger and frustration welled inside her. She turned away from her father's knowing gaze. She looked to the stands slowly filling with people. "I've rocked him in my arms," she said softly.

"Dani girl." Her father draped an arm around her shoulders and drew her close. Her body, as if tired of standing, swayed to his. She hadn't leaned on anyone for so many, long years. But her head now found her father's shoulder and rested for a moment. She knew he was right. It was only a matter of time.

Her father led her to a bench lining the walkway. She didn't protest but sat down, weary.

"I was watching you this morning," he said, his body still supporting hers. "I know you're happy, but how long can it last? How long before you want more?''

She shook her head. "This is more than I ever expected.''

"Then how long before your guilt gets the best of you and you have to tell the truth?''

Her eyes met his.

"Integrity," he said. "I don't know where you get it from—must've been your mother because it sure wasn't your old man—but you've got it...always did, always will. When you were no more than thigh-high, if somebody dripping in diamonds dropped a quarter in the dirt, you'd chase them halfway across the shed-row to give it back. Then, when they were so pleased by your honesty, they wanted to give it to you as a reward, you said no. And you never could tell a lie...unless it was to save your old man's sorry butt.''

She stared out at the people passing by, her lips pressed tight. Her father drew her to him. "I love you, Dani. C'mon back with me to Calder where it's warm and the palm trees sway at night like strippers.''

Dani straightened, breaking his hold. She shook her head. "I've been running my whole life. No more. I'm not leaving my son again. No one can make me leave him. I'm his mother.'' She willed the tremble out of her voice. The words came stronger. "I'm his mother.''

"You don't know what you're dealing with here. Let sleeping dogs lie.''

She shook her head.

"Do you think these people consider you anything

more than the stall mucker who cleans up after their prized ponies?''

''You don't know them.''

Her father stared at her. ''Yes, I do.''

''They're not like that.''

''No? So when Reid Hamilton learns you're the sweet young thing who slept with him after a few sips of champagne and some smooth talk and then sold him his own child—''

''It wasn't like that.'' Dani's hands balled into fists atop her thighs. Several spectators on their way to the stands glanced her way.

''You'll be causing a scene soon, Dani. That can't be good.''

''It wasn't like that,'' she insisted, her voice lower.

Mick leaned back, stretching his arms out along the back of the bench. He crossed his leg, his toe tapping the air to an imaginary beat. ''A child he doesn't even know is his own son,'' he continued, as if he hadn't heard Dani's denials. He tipped his head, lifted his face to the sun and closed his eyes. ''What a happily ever after that'll be, huh, Dani girl?''

''So you came all this way to give me some fatherly advice?''

Mick rolled his head to the side, squinted one eye open.

''What's in it for you this time, Dad?''

''I'm only looking out for your best interests, Dani.''

''And yours too, right?''

He turned his face back to the sun, his eyes closing

once more, his charming smile coming as easily as taking a breath. "Ah, I've missed you, Dani."

"I've missed you, Dad." She spoke the words rawly but sincerely. Not even her anger would deny him. Long ago, she'd learned to overlook her father's flaws in favor of his gifts. He was human, no more, no less than herself, than others.

His smile dissolved and such a sadness came to his features, she took his hand. "Dad."

He turned his head away. "He'd be lucky if you would have him. You know that, Dani?" He turned his head back to her. "Reid Hamilton would be a lucky man to be loved by the likes of you."

She shook her head, dropped her gaze to her father's hand in hers. "I've found my child." Her gaze lifted. "Be happy for me." She pressed her palm a little harder to his.

"I'm happy for you, darling. However, I'm also afraid for you. Afraid what's going to happen when you lose your baby boy again."

"It's not going to happen. I'm not giving my child up again."

Mick shoved his hands in his pants pockets, slumped lower on the bench, stared at the passing crowd. He sighed. "Maybe not. Maybe not."

She leaned over, kissed his coarse cheek. Without looking at her, he reached up, his hand finding the side of her face.

After a long moment, his hand dropped. He reached inside his jacket and pulled out the money clip. "Here," he said, peeling off several bills.

"No, no." Dani put her hands up. "I don't need your money."

"I know you don't need it, but I want you to have it."

She pushed away his hand. "I'm making a fair wage at Hamilton Hills. I have room and board. I've got everything I need."

Her father dropped the money into her lap. "Buy something for the boy." He turned away, pretending to watch the crowd.

She studied his profile as she folded the bills, tucked them into the front pocket of her chinos. "He inherited your smile, you know."

Her father heaved a sigh. "Let's just hope that's the only thing he inherited from me." Her father stood, still avoiding her gaze. "Well, I've got money to go and win, darling."

She looked up at him, shading her eyes from the sun. "So you'll be around for a while?"

He shrugged, smiling his old smile again as he turned to her. "You know me, darling. Depends on the odds." He opened his arms. "Come give me a hug and wish me luck."

She stood and hugged her father. "Wish me luck," she whispered, her face pressed to his. She drew back and looked at him, her hands resting on his chest. "You'll be in touch?"

His face sobered. He nodded. "And I know where to reach you, don't I?" He patted her hands. "It couldn't hurt for you to hang some garlic, Dani girl." He winked. "Couldn't hurt your horse either."

She laughed as he kissed her one last time. She watched him saunter off, jingling the change in his pants pocket, his steps quickening at the promise of one, two, three, maybe more payoffs, and, for a brief moment, beating the gods.

The horses for the first race were coming out. Dani didn't want to be alone with her thoughts, her father's dire predictions. She headed back to the barns to sit with Solstice.

The fifth race came. She looked for shade, trying to stay within its cool circle as she walked the colt to the receiving area. She kept her breaths steady and her touch calm. She cinched the girth on the saddle and let the irons down, hearing Smiley's low, soothing rumble behind her, giving last minute instructions to the jockey. Reid was silent. He was no longer smiling. The sharp lines of his brows were drawn together. His lips pressed tight. In the unfenced paddock, she passed the shank to the pony rider and stepped to the saddle. She laced her fingers and bent forward as the jockey in Hamilton Hills' gold-and-black silks came toward her. She waited until Reid's gaze came to her. She smiled and gave him a wink. His lips tipped up in a tiny curve. The jockey swung up, settled in. Dani laid her palm on Solstice's neck, then kissed the spot she'd touched. The bugle announcing the post parade sounded. The colt walked away. He was shining.

She was purposefully alone as she headed to the rail, then Reid was beside her, his steps matching hers. She hadn't heard him coming, yet she wasn't surprised when she turned and there he was. She looked behind

him for Smiley. The trainer wasn't there, and again
she looked at Reid without surprise. She knew why he
was here. He'd seen her secret with Solstice—the calm
that could touch the core of another, and so he'd come
to her now, needing it near him during this race. She
was no more than the garlic garlands strung over a
stall that her father spoke of. She kept her breaths
even, her steps steady and her gaze forward, smiling
with a self-confidence she would never admit didn't
exist. He took her arm above the elbow in a most
natural way, and she only stiffened a second as he
steered her toward the boxes. She had forgotten how
easily he seduced. No more than a look, a touch, a
name uttered and a woman believed she was all that
mattered.

They didn't talk during the post parade. She sat with
her hands folded in her lap, her feet tucked under the
seat, not daring to make a move or have a thought,
more silent than silence. He glanced at her once, and
her smile was serene. Then the horses moved to the
starting gate and Reid didn't look at her again.

The odds-on favorite was a California-bred gelding
readying for the stakes after impressive allowance
scores in Belmont. The line on Solstice in the *Form*
was "Woke up last time out to win at big odds. Pre-
viously stalled after an impressive maiden."

The horses moved into the starting gate. Dani's even
breathing didn't break as one by one the back gates
shut. She sat straight, still, composed of calm.

There was the silent beat before every start. Keeneland had no announcer. This was horse country and if

someone didn't know the barn's colors, the attitude was what were they doing inside the course's ivy-covered stone walls. The gates would clang open only to more silence. Dani smiled serenely.

Solstice broke, and there was nothing but this black beast bearing down. Ignoring his post position, he went wide as he headed toward the first turn. At the turn, he was still on the outside and very, very wide, falling back, falling back. Dani saw Reid's hands become fists atop his thighs. She looked away from the field to the finish line, all her focus now on that long thin line that from a certain position seemed not to even exist. She looked back to the colors and the animals and the movement and saw Solstice still on the outside but in the clear now and she suppressed her urge to lay her own cool palm on Reid's fist. It wouldn't be necessary. Solstice kicked in and was gaining ground with each stride. By the eighth pole, he was glued to the favorite's flank and still pouring on the speed into the stretch. Then he broke, his ears pinned, the jockey crouched against his neck, the horse's stride seeming to pass through his body like water. Solstice won by one and a half-lengths. Dani had smiled the whole time.

She turned to Reid. His hands uncoiled, and with a rich rightness, he again cupped his fingers an inch or so above her elbow to lead her to their horse and the winner's circle. She had taken a step when Reid's fingers tightened and he pulled her to him, and they clung together in celebration, the world emptying of all else.

Just as abruptly, they parted, hurried down to the track, Reid's fingers staying on her elbow.

Solstice came toward them glistening and blowing, muscle upon muscle still rippling. Dani saw the jockey's chin and cheeks streaked with blood. Reid's smile dissolved.

"He reared his head up in the gate and gave me a bloody nose," the rider told them with such a wide, pleased grin, everyone else smiled. Except Reid.

The jockey swung down off the colt, and Reid stepped forward to examine him, one hand clapped to the rider's shoulder. The jockey waved away the other man's worry. "Just a bit of a bump. Could happen to anyone. I'll clean up before pictures and be handsome as always." He patted the horse's long neck before handing the reins to Dani. "Helluva stretch drive, darling."

Reid gave the colt one more uncertain glance, but his expression eased as he shook the jockey's hand.

"C'mon, sweetheart," Dani crooned to the colt. "We'll get you to the winner's circle where you belong."

Reid stood to the side, discussing the race with the jockey and Smiley. That didn't mean he didn't see Solstice drop his head low against Dani's chest and go still as if listening for the woman's heartbeat. That didn't mean he didn't see the woman's hands fit around the animal's ears and stroke them as they slipped through her fingers like silk. It had become so he couldn't take a breath without being aware of the woman.

He could no longer attribute it to the woman's flashes of resemblance to another and no more. He couldn't blame it on the heady flush of success. He watched Dani and the horse walk toward the winner's circle. It was more. Much more. Watching her care for his colt, seeing her smile into a child's eyes, glance up, give that smile to him, he had become as bewitched as the animal.

Surely she had done little to cast her spell. Her beauty was quiet, almost androgynous, her clothes standard stable fare. He'd only seen her hair left free and lovely twice. Both times he remembered distinctly.

Brought together by Thoroughbreds, their backgrounds varied widely. He chided himself even as he had the thought, yet it was the truth. It didn't seem to matter. She had come and with her, desire. He didn't understand it—the yearning that could take a man, a woman. He knew few did. Still he wasn't comforted. Since Danielle, his brother's death, he hadn't allowed himself to need. Now a woman had come and need was all there was. Need as relentless as his quest to restore the farm, as potent as his vow to protect his mother and his brother's son, as great as his desire to heal a shattered family. Need as overwhelming as one night five years before.

They stood together in the winner's circle—the animal, the rider, the trainer, the owner, the groom—and had their picture taken. Later, when Reid saw the photo, he wasn't surprised to see he hadn't been smiling.

The ride back was short and noisy. Georgia brought Trey and met them in the barns.

"We won," Reid cheered, his spirits rising as soon as he saw the boy. He lifted the child high in the air, spinning him in a circle.

Dani watched the boy's head bend back and heard his laughter and laughed also. There was so much laughter in the barns that day.

It was an insignificant race, one that wouldn't even have been talked about years back when Derby wins and Breeder's Cups were the reasons for celebration at Hamilton Hills. Dani saw Georgia clap her hands together, her face flush with pleasure at Reid's news, and she knew how hard it had been for them these past years.

She looked to Reid, saw him spinning with their child, and thought of her betrayals. She wanted to turn away, ashamed, but she couldn't. The child and man bound her as tight as her narrow muscles. Reid held Trey up toward the sky, smiling into the child's eyes. He should know the truth, Dani thought. He deserved to know the child was his. His gaze dropped to her as if she had called his name, and she might have been no more than the air he breathed.

She had, once again, as always, fallen effortlessly in love.

She turned away. It was the joy of the win, the sound of her son's laughter that had made her light-headed and foolish. Still it hurt, wanting Reid, wanting Trey, and knowing neither one could ever be hers. She had been given one wonderful night with Reid, a night she knew would never be more than a brief, magical moment. Now she'd been given the gift of her son. She had no right to imagine more.

"We must celebrate," Georgia insisted.

"Mama, it was one small race. It's only the beginning of a long road."

"But a triumphant beginning nonetheless." Georgia spread out her arms and swayed to invisible music. "And it will be celebrated," she said in a voice that brooked no argument as she waltzed over to her son and held out her graceful arms for her grandson. She glanced over her shoulder at Solstice being fussed over in his stall. "Make sure that beautiful black colt gets extra oats tonight," she instructed as she danced off with Trey, "and have everyone come up to the house after supper, and we'll drink to the horses of Hamilton Hills."

"You heard her, men. Spread the word. Beers and shots of bourbon up at the house tonight," Reid said, his voice mildly amused as he watched his mother sashay toward the barn doors

"And cake and champagne for the ladies," Georgia added from the other end of the barn.

"That would be for you, Miss Dani."

Reid leaned against the side of the stall door, a light still in his silver eyes, a gentle smile on his face. She squatted down, checking Solstice's legs once more. "Thank you, no."

"Thank you, no?" The genuine surprise in his voice made her look at him.

"It's been a long day."

"Not as long as some." That smile came again, the one that once had stolen hearts all over the South. He reached over the stall guard, offering his hand to help her up. "Those wrappings look fine."

She had no choice but to dust off her hand against her pant leg and let him have it. For one second, there was the rightness of his touch. Then she took her hand back.

"I know it was only a minor race. And the bloody nose did nothing to allay my concerns about this animal's unpredictable behavior." He looked at Solstice. The colt widened his nostrils and blew out a breath. Reid smiled reluctantly. He looked at Dani.

"But my mother's right. It's a good beginning. You're part of it."

She looked into his eyes and could only think of her betrayal. She should tell him. The thought came to her again, stronger, irrational. She looked away, took a full breath. She looked back, met Reid's silver stare. She saw her son's eyes.

She also saw the man who had held her in his arms, touched her as if she were precious. A man who had had so much taken from him.

How much longer would she be able to look at that face and be silent?

Chapter Ten

She heard the laughter, saw the lights as she left the cabin. The radio was playing. The sun was low behind the ancient oaks. The stars and moon would soon bring dreams.

The day's mild temperatures had not yet dropped and people were clustered on the veranda or scattered about the lawn in small groups. Dani nodded to the other workers, stopping to retort to a teasing comment from one circle. She saw her son dancing across the veranda and, for a moment, was unable to respond to the jest. She saw Reid standing to the side, his tall, broad figure unmistakable. As if sensing her study, he turned and looked at her. Everything was different— the music, the guests, the circumstances. Yet it might have been that night five years ago.

She turned to the others surrounding her, her hand running over her smooth crown. Her hair was still damp from the shower and pulled back into a tight braid. She shouldn't have come. She would have a piece of cake, a sip of champagne and go back to the cabin. She chanced a furtive glance and saw a slender, blond-haired woman beside Reid. She looked away, calling herself a fool, as Cicely Fox's vaguely familiar feminine laughter floated out into the night.

On the porch, Reid stared into Cicely's bright eyes, lined with a chocolate color and shaded the blue of when day turns to night. She had come into town only today, had heard about the win and called to congratulate him. Georgia had insisted Cicely and her family come join them this evening. Cicely's grandfather, Harmon Fox, sat between Georgia and Otto now, sipping bourbon, smoking Otto's Havanas. Prescott was nearby talking to Smiley about the upcoming stakes. And Reid, remembering his vow to earnestly look for love, was looking down into Cicely's perfect face, trying very hard not to think about anything else but long, blackened lashes and lips that always seemed to smile. It wasn't until he saw Dani's thin, strong figure come down the winding path that he realized he'd been waiting and watching for her.

"He's a sly one, your boy there." Cicely's grandfather lifted his glass to Reid. "Stole my horse right out from under me." He took a sip, smiled at Reid over the rim.

"I believe in horse racing, we call it claiming, Harmon." Georgia smiled at her guest.

"Leave it to the track to give thievery a legitimate name. All I know, Georgia, is your boy here sees my colt known primarily for cowkicking, colic and being a one-turn *wunderkind,* looks right past all that disappointment and finds heart. He's got a good eye, your son. Just like his father.'' Harmon patted Georgia's hand. ''Your husband would've been proud of him.''

Georgia nodded, smiling at her son.

''And not only does he claim my colt to turn him into a champion, he steals one of my best grooms.''

Georgia smiled at Reid. ''You said it yourself—my son has a talent for finding heart. If you're hoping to get either one of them back, you're out of luck, Harmon. We've grown quite fond of Miss Dani, haven't we, son?''

''Miss Dani?'' Trey, pushing miniature cars across the porch's planks, looked up at his grandmother. ''Can Miss Dani play?''

''I'm sure she can be persuaded but it'd be nice if we brought her a piece of cake and a glass of champagne first,'' Georgia told the child, smoothing his hair as he came to her chair.

Trey shook his head. ''Dani likes milk better. Chocolate's best.''

Georgia glanced at her guests, chuckling.

''You've proven your point, Georgia,'' Cicely's grandfather said, ''That doesn't mean I forgive your son.'' He smiled at Reid.

''Goodness, you are like one big happy family here,'' Cicely observed, looking out at the stable workers on the lawn.

''Yes, if you'll excuse me…'' Georgia got up motioning for the men to stay seated as they started to rise. ''I'd better check on my other guests.''

Reid saw the amused look Cicely sent Prescott. Georgia saw it, too. ''Trey, come help Grandmamoo find Miss Dani and get her a big piece of cake. Maybe Miss Cicely would like to help us?''

Cicely looked at Georgia and Trey. ''Well, yes, I suppose so. That would be fun.'' She took a drink of champagne, gestured with her glass and said, ''Lead the way.''

Trey looked up at the woman, his silver eyes studying her. Cicely looked down at him, making her smile as bright as her eyes.

He gave her his hand. ''Okay, follow me, Miss Celery.''

''Isn't he just too adorable?'' Cicely cooed, her heels clicking as she tried to keep up with the boy.

''Easy on Miss Cicely now, Trey,'' Reid cautioned as the boy pulled her toward the steps.

He turned back to his other guests. Harmon eyed him. ''You're not considering stealing anything else of mine, are you, son?''

Reid saw the smile on the old man's face but understood the undercurrent of seriousness in his tone. ''Your granddaughter's a lovely woman, Harmon, but we're good friends, that's all.''

Harmon arched a brow. ''You better not let her hear you say that.'' He looked at Reid's empty glass. ''Pour yourself another two fingers and sit with me a minute.''

Reid picked up the bourbon decanter from the table and poured some into the other man's glass, then his own.

Harmon looked out across Hamilton Hills as he sipped his drink. ''You kept most of the land, I see.''

Reid understood. The track talk had confirmed the Fox stables were considering a move south. Now that the women were gone, Harmon was ready to talk business.

"All of the land," Reid told him. "I understand you're thinking about moving Fox Run Farm down this way."

Harmon's sharp glance told Reid they'd just rounded the first turn, and Reid had pulled out in front.

"Like I told your mother, your father would be proud of you." Harmon raised his glass in salute.

"Thank you, sir."

"You've had a rough time these past few years."

Reid sipped his drink. "We're coming along."

"Ever think about selling out?"

Reid looked out to the gentle roll of the rural savannah. "Not anymore."

The Fox family patriarch released a hearty laugh. "My granddaughter was right about you." Smiling, he pointed a finger at Reid. "She said you never took the easy road." He clinked his glass to Reid's. "I admire that."

"So that's what you're offering? An easy road?"

The old man shook his head, smiled as he brought his drink to his lips. "No such thing, son. No such thing."

DANI SAW her son coming down the steps, leading Cicely, and jealousy hit her like a single, low shot to her stomach. *He's my son,* she thought with a fierceness that surprised even her. She watched Cicely struggling to keep up with the child, taking quick, mincing steps in her narrow, short skirt. *He's my son.* Georgia leaned over to the boy and pointed at Dani. Trey looked, smiling when he spied her. Releasing Cicely's hand, he ran to her, his uncovered head gold in the half-light, his eyes silver suns. She squatted down to meet him.

He stopped before her, his narrow chest lifting with each breath. She held out her hand in hello. She brought her other hand up, clasping his in both of hers, making a cocoon for that small, precious hand.

She looked up, meeting Cicely's gaze, and feeling petty but victorious nonetheless, thought: *He's my son.*

She looked at the child. "I hope you saved a dance for me, darling."

"Good evening, Dani." Georgia came up and stood beside Cicely. "You know Cicely Fox, don't you?"

Dani released Trey's hand and straightened. "Hello, Miss Fox."

Cicely nodded. Dani knew she had no idea who she was nor did she care.

"I'm Dani Tate. I groomed for your grandfather before coming to Hamilton Hills." She didn't offer her hand nor did Cicely.

"She's the gem your grandfather was just scolding Reid for stealing away." Georgia smiled at Dani. She smiled back. Cicely looked from one woman to the other.

"Have you had some champagne and cake?" Georgia gestured to the table set up in the yard

"I'm fine," Dani assured her.

Georgia looked at her guest's empty hands. "C'mon, Trey. Let's go get Miss Dani some refreshments, and then, it's up to bed for you."

Trey automatically began to protest.

Dani put her hand on Georgia's forearm. "Let me."

"Dani, you're our guest tonight."

"Really, I wouldn't offer if I didn't want to. You stay here and entertain your guests."

"If you're sure—?"

Dani nodded. She squatted down to Trey once more. "What do you say, we have a little cake, and then up to bed with you?"

Trey considered the offer. "Chocolate milk with the cake?"

"What else?"

Dani and Trey looked up at Georgia. She smiled. "Milk's in the kitchen."

Dani stood and took her son's hand once more. "We'll just grab a bit of cake and bring it in there."

"He had his bath earlier, and as you can see, he's got his pajamas on. Just make sure he brushes his teeth well."

"Hear that?" Dani looked down at Trey. "Orders from headquarters, Captain."

Trey smiled and saluted. "Aye-aye, General." He kissed his grandmother and said good-night to Cicely and the others as they got their cake and headed toward the house.

They stopped on the veranda so Trey could say good-night to Reid and the other men. Reid saw her waiting by the sliding doors, balancing a piece of cake in each hand. "Dani?" he questioned as he came toward her. He looked out at the lawn for Georgia.

"I offered to take Trey up and tuck him in," she explained.

"Sit down, Reid," Harmon called from his seat. "I'm not going to steal her away from you." He smiled at Dani. "How's he treating you?"

"Fine, Mr. Fox."

"Good."

Trey pushed the sliding door back.

"Dani?" Reid stopped her as she stepped into the house. "Thank you."

She gave him a small smile and followed Trey down the hall to the kitchen. They made chocolate milk and ate their cake, the music from outside faint in the background.

"Parties are fun, huh?" Trey asked, shoving a hunk of cake in his mouth.

Dani smiled. "They're okay."

"Birthday parties are the best because you get presents."

"Is that so?" Dani brushed a smear of frosting off the child's cheek. She tasted her fingertip. "M-m-m-m, you're delicious."

Trey giggled. "Sweet as sugar, right?" He giggled some more.

"Sweeter," she assured him. "So, you've had some good birthday parties?"

"Yeah. Did you?"

"Did I what?"

"Did you have good birthday parties?"

She thought a moment. "I had one I remember." She stood and gathered the plates and glasses. "It was my eighteenth birthday."

"Did you get good presents?"

She turned and looked at her son sitting at the table. She smiled. "Oh, yes."

Dani wiped off the table and rinsed out the dishcloth in the sink. Turning back to the table, she found Trey standing on a chair.

"What are you doing, honey?"

He opened his arms to her. "I saved you a dance."

She smiled, wagged her finger. "You'll do anything to postpone going up to bed, won't you?" she said as she walked over to him.

He lifted his arms higher.

She looked into his eyes level with hers. "All right. But after this, we're dancing right up to bed, understand?" She tried to make her voice stern.

He smiled. Gathering him in her arms, she settled him on her right hip and humming to the faint music, circled with him around the kitchen. He leaned back his head, laughing. Dani was laughing too as they spun and dipped until they were breathless and dizzy.

She stopped, catching her breath. His head came up, his eyes bright. "Again."

"Are you kidding me?" She stood him on the seat of the chair. Their arms stayed linked. "Are you trying to kill me?"

They were only swaying now. "How 'bout we dance up to your bedroom?" She leaned him back in an exaggerated dip. "Although I must admit you dance divinely, young man."

He giggled as she brought his beautiful, bright face back up to her. "But I bet all the girls tell you that."

He shook his head, smiling.

"C'mon, now, don't be modest. Come here often?"

Trey looked around the kitchen. "Every day."

She heard the sweetness in her own laughter. She pressed her forehead to his, and they stared at each other cross-eyed. "So, you're one of those?" she said with a pretense of fear.

"One what?" He smiled wider, waiting for the answer.

"A dancing fool?" Her voice grew alarmed. "A disco duck?"

"A disco duck?" he repeated incredulously as they giggled and swayed and stared cross-eyed at each other with delight.

It was how Reid found them, giggling and swaying, their foreheads pressed together, their noses touching, the sight so charming, he stopped in the doorway to drink it in.

Dani hummed to the faint melodies drifting in. "Okay, little man, let's dance up to bed." Still Reid watched as she gathered the boy in her arms, the child tucking his head against her neck. Reid started into the kitchen when Trey said, "Dani?"

"M-m-m?" She brushed the hair off the boy's forehead.

"Love you."

Reid saw her body sag. Her hand reached, found

the table's edge and held on. He stepped toward her when her voice, hushed, breaking, stopped him. "I love you, too, baby boy."

She turned and saw Reid. He saw the tears on her face. He saw her fear.

"I didn't mean to scare you. We needed ice." He raised the bucket he held. "And more..."

His voice trailed off. She nodded, staring at him, shiny streaks on her face. Her eyes were big, sad, frightened. She looked no more than a child herself. What was her pain, he wondered?

"Here." He set the bucket on the table, reached for the child. "He must be heavy. Let me help you."

He gently took the boy from her. Her arms dropped, hung at her sides. Reid glanced at the child now snuggled against his shoulder. "He'll sleep tonight." He smiled at Dani.

She looked at the boy's profile. His eyes had already closed. "We were dancing." She sounded so beaten.

"I know." Reid touched her damp cheek. His fingertips brushed away her tears. She looked at him, still afraid.

"You'll make a wonderful mother one day." He leaned over, kissed her forehead lightly, then turned and carried Trey upstairs.

She sat down on the chair. Her hands clenched the wooden seat where Trey had stood in slippered feet seconds ago.

She couldn't hide the truth much longer. She couldn't lose her child. She should get up, go outside, say good-night, but indecisiveness seemed to have taken her movement, her reason. She heard Reid's steps coming down the stairs. She sat still. Her palms pressed to the warm wood seat as if this was all she had left.

He didn't look surprised when he saw her still sitting there. He smiled. "He's out like a light."

She nodded. She looked around the kitchen with its clean, straight lines, stainless steel appliances, counters that ran the width of the walls. She looked at Reid who watched her and smiled gently again. They might have been a couple—mother and father, husband and wife, partners, lovers, friends. Their child was safe, sleeping, dreaming in his room, and they had paused, acknowledging the end of another day. She looked away, the image of what was never to be so real, so near, she knew if she stood, her legs would buckle.

Reid came to her, pulled out a chair and sat beside her. She thought of the night in the barn, her cool hand on his shoulder, offering comfort. Now he wouldn't abandon her either. And though she knew how wrong all this was, she didn't want him to go. Still frightened, not knowing what she would say, do, she turned her head and looked at him.

His hand found hers holding tight to the wooden seat. Confusion formed on her features. His fingers curled around hers until her hand nested in both of his. She thought of a Thoroughbred's legs touched with the greatest of care. Right now she was being touched with that same great care.

"It's a wonderful thing—dancing." Reid smiled at her, his hands warm and dry around hers and his eyes much more than kind. She stared at him, becoming lost in that gaze.

"And those nights. Those nights when you dance and it's so right, you forget all else, only knowing there's such a thing as dancing and nights when it has to be done."

His smile was so tender. She looked at him and tried not to love him.

"I've had nights like that. And now Trey has had his first. Thank you." He leaned back in the chair. Smiling, her hand in his, he sat breathing in the silence that she knew was supposed to save her.

Chapter Eleven

Two days later Solstice threw Angel and broke the boy's arm. Reid drove him to the emergency room and threatened the doctor when he suggested it might be easier if Reid waited outside. Even after the bone was set and Angel brought back to the farm, Reid hovered over the teenager until Bennie finally told him to go home. He was making the boy and everyone else nervous. Accidents happen in this business, and Angel wasn't the first nor would he be the last horseman to be thrown, nipped, stepped on or kicked.

Reid left but didn't go to the main house. He went to Solstice's stall. Dani was there as if she'd been waiting for him.

Reid eyed the horse. Solstice saw the challenge in the man's gaze and returned it.

"He'll be sold," Reid said, his gaze never leaving the animal. "Until he goes, no one else is to ride him."

"You can't sell him," Dani protested, her voice equally resolute. "He just won two days ago. He'll win again." She offered Solstice a handful of hay from the net. Reid's gaze fell on her. She looked straight into his silver steel eyes. "Let me ride him."

"No one is to ride him," Reid repeated. "He's a wild card. I was wrong to bring him here."

"You brought him here because you saw something in him. It's still there. Remember Keeneland two days ago? And that last race he ran in Saratoga? He can do that again. And again. Give him his chance."

Reid's stare was so intense she was tempted to take several steps back. She didn't move. "It's easy to look at this colt and see only one thing trouble. But you looked at this colt and you saw something different, something more. You weren't wrong. It's still there." She glanced at the animal. "It's still there." She looked at Reid. "And you still see it."

He was quiet a moment. "And do you ever not see it?"

"No." Her answer was immediate.

"Let me tell you what I've seen—tantrums, biting, kicking, a jockey with a bloody nose, now a boy not more than sixteen with a broken arm. What's next? What if it's worse? What if…" His voice faded as he remembered another night when it had been worse.

"Finish feeding him and turn him out this afternoon." He walked away.

"Let me ride him."

He turned and fixed her in his dark stare. "No." He left, only a silhouette as he stepped into the sunlight.

Dani looked at the colt contentedly munching hay.

Solstice raised his head, looked back at her. Dani stared, seeing what she always saw, what Reid still saw although he wouldn't admit it. She went to the tack room.

A few minutes later she led Solstice, saddled and bridled, out the barn door, aware of every movement, every muscle of her body, the horse's body. Reid was talking to Smiley at the training track, undoubtedly telling him his plans to sell Solstice. Their backs were turned to her but as the gelding they were watching finished his workout and trotted off the track, they turned and saw Dani swinging herself up into the thin saddle.

Reid's face turned to anger. Dani's heart faltered as she met his gaze. He stepped toward her when Smiley laid a hand on his arm and said something that stopped him. Dani stared back at him, her expression controlled while inside she was anything but serene.

Smiley came forward, meeting Dani as she approached the track. Solstice arched his thick neck, raised his head high, ready. ''Do you know what you're doing?'' Smiley asked, laying a calming hand on the horse's cheek. The trainer, too, had seen the champion in this animal.

Dani nodded, lying.

''This may be his last run here.''

She nodded. She'd known it even before she'd turned toward the tack room.

''And even if everything goes perfect, this may be your last ride at Hamilton Hills, too.''

She had known if the horse went, she would've also

been expected to go. She had never considered if the horse stayed, she still might be asked to leave. She looked past Smiley, met Reid's eyes. Recklessness.

"Gallop him easy," Smiley instructed. "Nothing more. Don't fight him but don't let him take control either. And don't make me regret this." Dani saw hope in the older man's stern expression.

"Thanks, Smiley." She wrapped her hands around the straps and took hold. Solstice tucked his chin. She looked the length of the shining dark neck in front of her and not at the man standing at the oval. She felt the coiled proud power of the animal. The same strength and determination was in the line of Reid's stance as he stood at the rail. She felt the horse's calm, steady sway beneath her and nestled low, folding herself against the animal's neck, pressing her heartbeat to the sway, hoping to contract its rhythm. From between the horse's ears, she saw Smiley stand beside Reid. The trainer would never openly oppose the owner's decision but she knew he was now offering his advice in that low easy tone she had learned.

Solstice flicked his ears as if trying to listen to the conversation in front of him but Dani knew from the horse's long strides, he was just anxious to run. "Soon, boy, soon," she whispered.

She led him onto the training track. Not once did she look at Reid.

"Start him once around with a slow trot," Smiley told her.

Dani nodded. She knew it was a test. She released the reins until Solstice launched into a high trot, then kept a strong hold on the straps, feeling movement, muscle and now through the leather, mouth. The animal braced against her in protest but he gave her once around the oval and pulled up when instructed to where Reid and Smiley stood at the rail. She knew they'd both seen her premature smile before she remembered to wipe it off her face.

Neither man commented. This was a track where, like all tracks, the rule was unpredictability. Dani knew it as well. But these two men hadn't just touched power in their hands, in their hearts.

Beyond Reid and Smiley, Dani saw Bennie leading the bay filly out of the barn to turn out in the pasture.

"This time, try a little canter," Smiley said, his features always solemn, his tone businesslike. "A slow canter. No more. Hold him."

She loosened the reins. She didn't cluck. It was her silence Solstice always understood. He moved forward. By the first turn, he'd moved into the sweet, soothing speed of the canter. Dani felt the pull on the reins at the second turn but carefully drew them in, holding Solstice to the easy, rocking rhythm. At the third turn, she saw another exercise boy had joined the men at the rail. Bennie was watching as he walked the filly. Dani's gaze shifted back to the men at the rail. She was trying to decipher Reid's expression when she felt Solstice switch leads and dig in, lengthening his stride. She didn't fight it as he'd expected, as Smiley had told her and Reid had feared. She looked away from the men, leaned into the power, let it fill her. She felt the four beats of a gallop and steady certainty of the steps beneath her. The animal surged, and she bridged her reins and pressed into his thick neck, her body stretching and folding with the rhythm of the horse. All was wind now and movement, a strong wave, the only noise the steady accelerating beat of hooves. She couldn't see except for blurs, could only feel heat and the inevitable rush forward and the joy rising, seeking expression. Still she stayed silent while inside her she heard her own voice sounding, echoing like the wind.

How many times they went around, she wasn't sure. All she knew was she felt the first lessening of power and knew Solstice was satisfied and happy. The strides slowed to a canter, trot. The muscles beneath Dani were trembling, continued to tremble even as Solstice walked toward the stretch and the poker-faced men at the rail.

She pulled up alongside the rail.

"What was that?" Reid asked.

Now Dani realized her muscles were trembling too, as exhilaration filled her, seeming to set her free. She reared back her head, releasing a full laugh, silence no longer necessary. She could feel the early autumn sun on her face and still taste the sweetness of the wind. "What that was, gentlemen, was pure heaven."

Reid looked up to the smiling, flushed face tipped to the sun, the delicate green eyes half-closed and saw the face, the woman, a moment he remembered. He squinted, trying to bridge the image with reality. But he only saw the woman above him; that face that he'd seen once before like this—ethereal, triumphant, taken with pleasure. Danielle DeVries. Dani Tate. Dani Tate. Danielle DeVries.

They'd become one and the same.

He closed his eyes to clear his mind. Hadn't he experienced the same illusion with the horse? Hadn't he looked at the black colt and seen Aztec Treasure, felt the shudder of fear and sadness shake him? Wasn't that, most of all, why he'd bought the horse? Had he become so desperate to relive that night, solve its riddle, he was now doing the same thing to this woman? Otto and the others were right. He had become obsessed.

He opened his eyes. The others were looking at him puzzled, waiting for him to say something. The images of that long-ago night were like a kaleidoscope, some sharp and defiant, some blurred and unformed, all changing and unreal. He looked at the woman above him, painting her in twilight now with bared shoulders, sweet laughter and features highly defined with colors and shadows. Was it her? Or was it his desire? God, let it be her. He didn't know. He didn't know. The others were still staring, waiting for him to speak, when he heard his own name yelled with the franticness he felt inside.

He turned to the summons. Maria was running toward him from the house, her outstretched arms flapping above her head. "It's your mother, Reid. Your mother."

All thought left Reid's mind as he ran, becoming as the animal he'd just seen—pure speed.

Smiley followed right behind. Bennie too handed

the filly off and ran to the big house. Dani wanted to go too, but knew it wasn't her place. She bathed and walked Solstice until he was cool, shuddering when she heard the wail of the ambulance. Silently she prayed for Georgia.

She was filling Solstice's water bucket when Bennie came back to the barn, his face looking older, tired. "Her heart," is all he said, shaking his head.

Georgia's wonderful warm heart. Dani gritted her teeth, not letting the tears form.

"Reid went with her in the ambulance. Smiley followed in Reid's car. He'll call as soon as there's any news."

She nodded. "How's Trey? He wasn't with Georgia when it happened, was he?"

"No, thank sweet Jesus. Maria said he was in the parlor watching television. Georgia was with Maria in the kitchen when the attack came. Nothing a child needs to see. He was scared when he heard all the commotion but Reid told him his grandmother was just feeling a little sick and they were taking her to the doctor to make her all better. He seems okay. Maria's with him now."

"I could help. I could stay and help take care of Trey until Reid gets home."

Bennie nodded. "That'd be fine. Reid will probably be awhile."

"I can take care of him as long as needed." *Forever,* she thought. She hurried to finish her work and go to her child.

She found him in the house's huge kitchen, eating

cookies and being fawned over by Bennie's wife. She took him outside, to the upper pastures to laugh at the yearlings' play, to the stables to handfeed Solstice and the other Thoroughbreds and watch his face break into laughter as the horses snuffled his tender palm. He was a miracle, this boy. Her son.

It was when she brought him in to wash up for supper, he asked when his grandma was coming back?

She sank to her knees, level now with those questioning silver eyes. "You remember a few weeks ago when the big black horse, Solstice, was sick."

Trey nodded, drawing his lips together and studying Dani.

"Well, your grandmamoo was feeling a little sick like Solstice, so she went to see a special doctor who can make her all better. Sometimes, that takes time though."

"When's she coming back?" he asked again, the concepts of death and serious illness thankfully foreign to this four-year-old.

"Well, that depends on what the doctor says."

Trey's expression was thoughtful. Dani was smiling, trying not to let her own concern reveal itself. Still he must have sensed her worry because he reached over and pressed his palm to her cheek. She couldn't speak, could only cover that small, soft hand with her own. *I'll never leave you again,* she silently vowed.

That night, Trey fell asleep on her lap as she read him a story. Unwilling to let him go yet, she sat in the rocker beside his bed, cradling the comfortable weight of his body against hers as she rocked her child. Smi-

ley had called after supper. Georgia's artery to her
heart had been blocked but they'd performed an an-
gioplasty without complications and she was out of
recovery and resting in her room. If all went well, the
doctors said she would be released in a day or two.
Smiley would drive Reid home later that evening.

Dani gave silent thanks as she rocked her son—
thanks that Georgia would be all right, thanks for her
child in her arms right now. She watched her son
sleeping. She had already missed a lifetime of nights
holding him. She would miss a lifetime more.

She looked at her son. Once more she couldn't help
wish that she, this boy, the boy's father were truly a
family, bound not by betrayal but by love.

She closed her eyes, gently rested her cheek against
the child's crown, trying to remember it all, the even
wash of his breath, his hair soft as sun against her
cheek, the sweet calm of him asleep in her arms, the
happiness, the yearning. So lulled, she herself fell
asleep, her head bowed to her son's.

Reid found them like that, curled together as if
mother and child, and the day swelled and threatened
to overtake him. He stared at the woman as he struggled to turn back any emotions. He thought of that
spring night and now saw Dani clothed in emerald
satin, her hair colored russet, her mouth a rich wine
red. He remembered her this morning astride the colt,
triumphant and beautiful as the woman of five years
ago. Once more he was lost between the past and the
present.

He studied her sleeping profile, still not sure who

she was. Not sure of anything this moment. Only knowing he wanted her. Only knowing he had wanted a woman this way just once before and that he had vowed he would never want again that badly.

He ran his hands over his face. It was the hour, his mother's illness, Angel's accident, this woman's resemblance to another. Still he dropped on his knees before her and knew nothing but need.

She woke as soon as he laid his hand on her arm. She blinked, her eyes adjusting, taking him in. He held a finger to his lips, signaling her to be quiet. He stood and gathered Trey in his arms, pressed his lips to the boy's forehead and for a moment, couldn't move with the sheer sweetness of such a simple act. He carried the child to his bed with the spaceship sheets and covered him up. He turned to see Dani standing by the rocker, watching him. Again he was struck by sweetness. Wanting rose within him, rich and bold and true. He saw Dani. He remembered the woman he'd known one night. He knew his need and his fear then and now. He couldn't afford vulnerability. The risks were too great. He had to protect himself. He held her solemn gaze a second longer, then motioned for her to follow as he started toward the door.

He didn't speak and walked several steps ahead of her so she saw only his back, the pride and power he carried in the lines of his body. He'd been called away before he could reprimand her about riding Solstice. He was still angry, and she deeply regretted causing him any more trouble on a day already full with crisis.

She followed him down the hall. They were halfway

down the stairs that led to the back of the house before he finally spoke.

"Thank you for taking care of Trey." His voice was polite, remote. His back was still to her.

"You don't need to thank me. How is she, your mother?" she whispered, although they were far from Trey's room.

"Resting."

Even beneath the tight tone, she heard the weariness. "You should get some rest too," she urged.

"I'm going back to the hospital as soon as I shower and change. Otto is there with her now."

Worry rose within her. "Everything is okay, isn't it? She's going to be—"

He turned with a look that stopped her words. "My mother is fine," he said as if defying death to come once more to Hamilton Hills.

She nodded, agreeing, reassuring. He continued down the steps, and she followed, feeling the gulf widening, a gap more than physical. She knew those moments of openness, closeness between them he now thought of with contempt. This morning she had betrayed him. She stared at that strong back. This morning had been the least of her betrayals.

"How was Trey?" he asked as they neared the bottom of the stairs. She heard voices coming from the kitchen.

"Good as gold. He asked about Georgia of course. I told him she wasn't feeling well but the doctors were making her better and she'd be home soon. He seemed to accept that."

Reid nodded. They reached the first floor. From the kitchen Dani recognized the low carry of Smiley's voice. Bennie and his wife had also waited for Reid to return from the hospital, keeping a pot of coffee on and food warm.

Dani stopped. Reid was halfway down the hall before he realized she wasn't following him. He looked back at her questioningly.

"I'm just going to say a quick good-night to the others, then go to the cabin." She was giving him a chance to punish her for her actions that morning.

He stepped toward her. His gaze seemed to go beyond skin and bone until she yearned to look away.

"I'm sorry I caused you trouble today." She broke the silence of his silver stare.

His face was so closed. Here was the man that had been born that night five years ago. Not in her arms, no, but later, in the barn where they'd said he'd been found, holding his brother's body, his eyes dry. The man who'd borne the rumors after, the suspicions surrounding the horse's injury, his brother's presence in the barn, the farm's precarious financial state.

The man who bore it all still.

"But I'm not sorry I did what I did."

She watched one corner of his mouth crook upward with amused reluctance. It was far from a smile. Not even half a smile. Still, to Dani, it was a most wonderful gift.

"And you'd probably do it all over again, too, wouldn't you?" he asked.

She looked up into those silver lights. "Yes."

Now the other corner of his mouth quirked upward. Dani knew such a simple curve shouldn't elicit such response, but she said one more silent prayer of thanks today. She straightened her body that had unconsciously curved toward him. If she began to believe again with her heart, she would lose everything.

He rubbed his brow. His features turned stern. "You pissed me off today, you know that."

"Yessir, I know that." She wasn't sure what was to come.

He studied her. What she didn't know was she had also made him smile for the first and only time that day.

He shook his head, chuckled, and she was lost.

"Smiley said you have good hands."

"But I'm too long in the leg."

"You'll be riding Solstice in the mornings from now on."

He saw her surprise. "I'll still groom him too, won't I?"

He chuckled again, the sound so pleasant. "I don't know anyone else who wants him. C'mon." He tipped his head toward the kitchen, "I'll buy you a cup of coffee."

A smile now came to Dani's face too as they walked together down the long hall.

Chapter Twelve

Reid heard soft voices as he came to the hospital room. He saw Georgia awake, propped on the pillows like a queen. Otto sat in a chair at her bedside, his hand resting on the side rails as he leaned toward Georgia. His mother looked over as Reid came through the door. She smiled, reaching out her hands to him. He set down the overnight case he'd brought and went to the other side of the bed, where the bags feeding her hung on a pole. He took her reaching hands in his, their veins and bones thin but their grip still strong. He leaned down, careful of the snaking tubes and kissed her. He straightened, smiled at her. Her hands still held his.

"What are you doing up?" His voice was hushed also. "You're supposed to be resting."

Georgia looked down the length of her prone body. "What do you call this? Doing the cha-cha?"

"How do you feel?" The worry crept into his voice despite his effort.

She squeezed his hands. His own grip tightened in

response. "I'm going to be just fine, honey. Don't you worry about me. Just a clogged pipe but now everything's flowing like the Mississippi after the spring thaw."

The white gown, pale sheets, wan light had brought a delicacy to her unadorned, unclouded face, the illness making her nothing if not more beautiful with her ivory translucent skin and her gold-blond hair piled high off her smooth forehead.

"It's you who hasn't slept." She had studied him also. "Have you?"

He looked away, ignoring her question. He saw tubes, a computerized monitor. "I brought you your things." He nodded toward the overnight bag and looked back at her. He couldn't let go of her hands.

"Thank you, sweetheart. How's our boy?"

Reid smiled. "He was sound asleep in Dani's lap when I got home. Maria and she are taking good care of him. You don't have to worry."

"I'm not worried. He adores them both. As do I." Her face sobered. "I don't want him to see me like this. I don't want to scare him." She closed her eyes. Reid glanced worriedly at Otto.

"She goes in and out," he said. "She's still pretty groggy from all the medication."

"But I can still hear you, my good friend," Georgia whispered, although she didn't open her eyes.

Otto smiled at Reid, shrugging his shoulders in surrender. Reid saw the weariness in the old man's face. "Otto, go get some rest. I'll be here."

The other man looked at Georgia resting peacefully,

beautiful and fragile. Reid knew it was the sheer angelic quality of her face, the frailty of her body that made it impossible to school deep emotions. He saw the rare helplessness in Otto's face.

Otto pushed his bulky frame up from the chair, his figure shadowing Georgia's still form. "Perhaps I will take care of a few things, then come back." He gazed down at Georgia.

Her eyes didn't open, but her one hand released Reid and searched until she found Otto's hand still grasping the bed rail. "Be a love and bring me back a medium rare sirloin and a pitcher of apricot sours."

Otto leaned forward to kiss her cheek. "Anything you want, Georgie. You know that." He straightened, looked at Reid. The helplessness was still in his eyes.

"You can reach me anytime on the cell phone," Otto told him.

"Go home, Otto," Georgia ordered.

"I'm going, I'm going," he promised, casting one last look at her. Georgia opened her eyes, smiled and gave him a wink.

Mother and son watched the man leave, then looked to each other. Against the bland surroundings, the twinkle in Georgia's eye was bold.

"You know, I fancied myself in love with him when we were young?"

Reid smiled. "I always suspected."

"He's lucky I met your father when I did or I might have made him marry me. But then your father came along and it was all over for me."

She smiled wistfully, her gaze going beyond her

son. "No one had ever made me feel like your father did. God, it was glorious." She squeezed her son's hands, her gaze returning to him. "That's what I wish for you."

He thought of Dani. He thought of a woman, a night five years ago. He knew Otto's helplessness.

His mother looked at him a long moment, then closed her eyes. Reid thought she'd drifted off until he heard her say, "The funny thing is, if it wasn't for Otto, your father and I might not have married. Did you know that?"

Reid knew the story well but he said, "Really?"

She opened her eyes, but she saw the past. "Your father's mother had been waging a campaign since the first moment she met me to convince him I wasn't the 'right' girl to marry. After we announced our engagement, she only became more determined to see the marriage didn't happen. A week after the announcement, your father confesses he's having second thoughts. We had a huge, horrible fight, and I told him to take his coveted Hamilton seed and stick it in his car."

Reid always smiled at this point. Today was no exception.

"When Otto heard what happened, he got so angry, he found your father and, well, they had an awful brawl, with your father, I'm afraid to say, bearing the brunt of it. Otto always said he merely knocked some sense into the man. All I know is that night, your father came and got me and we eloped. Your grandmother never forgave any of us. And poor Otto got locked up in the county jail until we got back and your father bailed him out and convinced your grandmother to drop the assault charges.''

She paused, but Reid knew that wasn't the end yet.

''But while Otto was in jail, one of the public defenders took a liking to him—seems Otto reminded the man of himself at that age and so forth. The man became Otto's mentor. Otto became a lawyer. And I got the man I loved.''

She smiled at her son. ''Now, you've heard that story enough that I'll expect you to get it right when you tell it to my great-grandchildren.'' Her smile turned stern. ''Providing you ever marry.''

He patted her hands with the sea blue veins. ''S-h-h. You rest now.''

She smiled, not fooled by her son's attempt to end the conversation, but changing the subject anyway. ''Otto and I—we both started out a long way from where we are now, didn't we?''

''Yes, you did.'' Reid patted her hand again.

''My family might have been poor, but there was one thing we were never without—love. Not so with Otto's family. Otto…'' She paused. Her silver eyes turned sad as if they saw too much. ''Let's just say, Otto wasn't loved.'' She looked at her son and away from memories. ''Even now, when he looks in the mirror, he doesn't see the man he's become. He sees only a young skinny boy that nobody loved.''

The sadness stayed in Georgia's eyes. ''My parents

and I tried to help—we were his family then.'' She looked at Reid. ''We're his family now.''

Her voice was groggy. Her eyes closed. ''But how much he missed by hanging on to the past.''

Reid gently let go of his mother's hands to smooth the sheet across the bed. ''You rest now, Mama. You're tired. We'll talk later.''

''The saddest part is...'' Her voice was even softer, slower. ''He learned so well how much love could hurt, no one was ever able to teach him that love could heal.''

Reid watched his mother's features relax. Soon he heard the deep breaths of sleep. He thought of death and life, hurting and healing. Love. Desire. He thought of Dani who'd come to Hamilton Hills and could quiet a colt, charm a child, make Reid smile in sadness. He thought of the other woman he remembered whenever he looked into Dani's eyes. Which woman did he desire? Did it matter? Wasn't the feeling as strong and as strange now as it had been five years ago? He took his mother's hands once more and could not let go.

IT WAS LATE when he got home. The house was dark, sleeping. He found Dani at the kitchen table as if he'd known all along she'd be there. Her cheek rested on her folded arms but, as soon as she heard his steps, her head jerked up. Lines creased her skin. The unawareness of sleep lingered in her eyes. She jumped up, scrubbing her hands across her face.

''Sit.'' He placed his hand on her shoulder. ''Sit.''

She sank back down into the chair without protest. His hand lingered on her shoulder.

She rubbed her eyes. "I must've drifted off. I'm sorry."

"Don't apologize." He pulled out a chair and sat beside her. "It's late. I couldn't bear to leave her until I was sure she was sleeping. Still I suspect she was faking just to get rid of me." He smiled and hoped she would too. She didn't disappoint him.

"How is she?"

"She's coming home tomorrow possibly."

"Reid, that's wonderful." Her hands clasped his and just as swiftly pulled back.

His hands grasped each other. "Trey was good for you?"

"An angel. But he'll be happy to have Georgia home."

"He won't be the only one."

She stood again, her hands on her denim-covered thighs. "It's late. I've got to go. Maria left you a plate in the refrigerator. She said to just pop it in the microwave for a minute or two."

He stood too, so near, he touched her with each breath. "I ate at the hospital."

She looked up into his face to tell him good-night. He looked battle-scarred and beaten. She saw a solitariness as deep and startlingly real as her own. All she had to do was reach out her hand, touch him, and, for that moment, each would have relief.

"Good night then." She was almost past him when

his hand caught her wrist. She kept her gaze on the doorway.

"Stay." His voice was hoarse.

He had asked. How much strength it had taken to mutter that one word. They both knew it. She turned her head to look at him. He met her gaze. His hand clung to her wrist. He was scared. So was she. She saw the fear. She also saw the need, wanting, desire. She felt it deep within her, the dull throbbing, the swollen heat, the tightening of muscle, the loosening of the heart.

She heard his plea.

He waited, so still. Her answer would either redeem or destroy. Which would it be? she wondered as she curled her fingers into his and whispered, "Yes."

He covered her lips with his, the kiss gentle, careful and, all the more, sweetly arousing. He looked at her, desire darkening his eyes as his hands trailed lightly across her face, her throat, down her arms as if she were unreal. Her body began to bend to him as his lips followed the path of his fingertips, grazing her shoulders, the hollow of her neck, finding her mouth again in a gentle caress that made her reach for him. He threaded his fingers through hers and lifting her hand, pressed a kiss to her palm before leading her down the hall, up the stairs, to his room. So steady were their steps, so even their breaths this time, she thought. As if over the past five years, they had learned so much and become wise. She stepped into his bedroom. She didn't move, her eyes adjusting to the darkness. He closed the door behind them, came and looked at her, his eyes, those silver moons that seemed to see her as no other did. He smiled, and she had to touch the rise of his cheek, skim her fingers to the line of his hair.

"Dance with me," he said.

She smiled. Five years, and they had learned nothing but this.

He slipped his arm around her waist, gathering her to him. He took her hand, tucking it to his chest, and, in his touch, she knew he would take care with her. There was no music except within them, and little movement, a step forward, back. They stood together, their bodies swaying. She placed her hand on the curve of his neck, looking into his eyes. Her other hand slid to the strength of his back. Her head lay down on his shoulder. Her cheek pressed to his collarbone, and she swayed, wishing she wore silk once more and smelled of spring.

His lips found the length of her throat, worked their way to her mouth, again softly seeking, pulling her slowly, fully into the kiss, their bodies waltzing to the slow churn of their blood. His arms wrapped around her as the kiss lengthened, and she placed her palms again to his cheeks, her fingertips feathering across his brow. She had yearned for him for so long. One more time, she would give him, take for herself. She tasted his mouth. Tomorrow she would remember this could not be.

He lifted his head, his silver eyes on her as she caressed the sides of his face. He reached up, pressed her palm to his cheek, then taking her hand in his, brought her to his bed. His hands on her shoulders, he eased her onto the edge of the bed and sat beside her, gently turning her to the side so her back faced him. From behind her, his hands slid across her shoulders, down her spine, his fingers finding her hair, loosening it from its tight band. Gently he unweaved her braid, and spread her hair across her shoulders, combing it softly down her back with his fingers, lifting it in his hands to bury his face in its luxuriant length. Her eyes closed, her head dropped back, free now.

His fingertips circled the offered curve of her throat, his touch idle, the nape of her neck pressed to the round of his shoulder. Her hair spilled across his arms. He ran one hand lightly down her throat, then the other, a man as schooled in touch as she. She heard the moan inside her, and then, outside her, so strong, she opened her eyes as it released as if to see it vibrate in the air around them, a haze of pleasure rising. His hands moved down, fingers skimming the soft sides of her breasts, sliding to her waist, slipping beneath the hem of her shirt to rub the thick skin of his thumbs and palms across her belly. The back of her head pressed into the hard stone of his shoulder as her head turned, her mouth finding the tender underside of his jaw. Strong bone beneath her nape, sweet flesh beneath lips.

His hands drew upward, smooth, dry, seeking, as if touch alone could tell him everything about her. She stretched, arching her back, waiting, her breath warm, rapid on his throat. His palms curved to the swell of her breasts. His thumbs brushed their puckered tips, his rhythm never changing, consistent, making her, making him, wait, want.

He shaped the curve of her waist once more, his hands gathering her T-shirt and lifting it over her head. The flat of his palm smoothed the flat of her stomach, taunted the soft rounds of her breasts. He unfastened her bra, sliding it off her shoulders. Her breasts budded with desire in the cool light as he fondled their fullness, the skillful brush of his fingers causing her body to tremble, strain. There was the intimate whisper of his lips against her throat, her ear, the soft run of his tongue, the deep draughts of her breaths. His hands moved down, forming her to his hard warmth. He found her waistline, unsnapped her jeans. She lifted her hips and pushed the pants down, kicked them off, smiling at her own impatience. She covered his hands caressing her hips and pressed them into her flesh. He laughed softly, sweetly. She smiled as he slid out from behind her to lay her down gently. He stretched out and lay beside her, the warmness and the desire and the overwhelming rightness flowing back and forth between them now.

He rolled to one side, leaned over her, those hands, those fingers touching her face tenderly, attentively across her brow, the planes of her cheeks, resting on her lips to outline the smile she realized was still there. His gaze focused on those lips as if he'd never known a mouth before, his fingertips tracing its circle, moving to her chin, her cheeks, his touch warm and moist as he soothed her skin. She closed her eyes and drew his face roughly down to hers, her open mouth moaning, moving into his as their lips met. He lay full upon her now, the heat of his body coursing down the length of hers. His mouth turned hard, hungry as his tongue slipped inside her lips and filled her, thrusting greedily, drinking deeply, his thumb rubbing deliciously back and forth across a taut nipple. His opened mouth drew down her flesh, bathing her in moist warmth, suckling her skin, the soft, full weight of her breasts, the taut tips of her nipples. His hands explored the lines of her waist, her hips, her thighs, drawing her closer until all conscious thought left her, leaving only his touch, his taste, his heat, her need, her demand.

He wrapped his arms around her, and they rolled until she was on top of him, their arms still holding each other tight. She used her weight, her mouth, her tongue to move deeper into him, reawakening to the wonder of this flesh, this man, a fury taking her, born from his skilled caresses, his masterful touch.

She unbuttoned his shirt, her mouth following her fingers, kissing, nibbling, suckling, sliding with parted lips across his skin. She leaned forward, her hair falling on his shoulders, his face as she kissed him full on the mouth. With a groan, he rolled her onto her back once more. He stood, undressed quickly and went into the bathroom. He returned, naked, with more beauty than the usual measure of man. He lay down beside her, drawing the coverlet over them, his arms pulling her to him. As he'd come out of the bathroom, she'd seen the thin sheath of protection stretched across his maleness. They had learned something during the past five years, after all.

He touched her face, her breasts, her belly. She was already trembling when his hands cupped her, stroked her, the flesh beneath his touch quivering as she lifted her hips and pressed her pelvis to his palm, thrusting against his fingers. With a gasp, she released into wave upon wave of pleasure, her body sinking deep into softness. Lost in sensation, she reached for him, drew him atop her, herself sinking, sinking. She wrapped her arms around him, finding him hard and heavy and smooth and hot as she stroked him. He slid like silk inside her. Her cry moistened his solid chest. She was melting all around him as he went farther and farther inside her to the very core of her. He placed his warm, caring hands on her face. She breathed in his strength and his sweetness, went to where he was inside her and dissolved. She was no more than the man within her.

She heard her name breathed again and again above her, as if calling her home, and then, in a final release of ecstasy and reverence, she heard, "Danielle."

Even in euphoria, her lies mocked her.

She turned her head into the pillow, closed her revealing eyes, uncertain if she had actually heard the name or had imagined it, her own guilt finally been given voice.

Fear kept her face turned away from him, her head pressed into the pillow, her eyes shut. Did he know the truth now? They lay joined, his weight wonderfully heavy on her, and she so small and full, her heart dense with him. Had their intimacy finally revealed what she alone knew, what her sudden movements, her glances, her expression might have unconsciously hinted at before? They lay together, whole, she not breathing, eyes shut, and not sure what she wanted the answer to be.

He shifted his weight to the side, afraid he was hurting her. Still he stayed inside her, unable to leave her yet. He had called her Danielle. It was her name. It was also another's. A coincidence, he'd dismissed along with his other confused desires to make the two separate women one. He looked at the woman turned from him now, her eyes closed, her expression closed, his emotions for her gliding through him, dizzying. Even as he damned his confusion, dismissed it as only obsession, he couldn't determine which woman he had really made love to, so hard had it become to separate his fantasy from the reality, so compelling had his desire become for both. And so, without forethought, in a moment without control, he had uttered that single name which joined both women, and for one breath, had felt himself whole once more.

His head dropped down.

She felt his breath by her ear, his mouth on her skin. She had to know. She turned her head, opened her eyes to look at him. She would never be more exposed. "You called me Danielle." She didn't know if it was a question or a statement.

"Yes."

She wasn't angry. How could she be angry? She knew the woman he made love to. And she was her.

"It's a beautiful name. No one ever calls you that?"

"Not since my mother died." Except once, now twice, she amended. Her breath held.

"I'm sorry."

She shook her head. He owed her no apology.

"May I call you Danielle?"

It was such a formal request, said so politely and with much reserve, although they lay naked and joined as intimately as possible. The absurdity struck her, then him, with a smile.

"Yes, you may," she said in the same formal tone although her smile turned wicked as she reached low to caress him and remind him of the intimacy they shared. She watched his eyes close, the sensuality deepening on his features, his smile remaining, and herself suddenly grateful the mood had turned silly. *Give us this little laughter,* she asked selfishly. There will be none after. Even before she had heard the name murmured, Danielle, she had known, had always known. She could lie to him no longer. Soon she would tell him the truth.

He moved his mouth to her shoulder to her neck, down to one rosy-tipped breast, already hardening with anticipation. He raised his head, still lazily smiling at her, such a newfound bright boyishness in the dark sensuality of his eyes. She was suddenly overcome with him.

"May I?" he asked properly.

She smiled, his body long and warm on hers, himself so deep in her heart, she felt it tremble. She brushed the hair from his forehead and said like a schoolmistress, "Yes, you may," continuing the game.

He bent his head, his mouth tasting her slowly, his eyes closing, her eyes closing so all that existed was the slow pull of his mouth and the fine trembling throughout her. It was so quiet, no thoughts of truths to be told later, pleas to be made, bitterness and anger to be expressed. All was quiet as her hands tangled in his hair and pulled him close.

After, she lay on her back and feigned sleep. He lay beside her, his arm stretched across her chest. Gradually his breaths deepened and his arm slipped, dropped to her side. She studied him, making sure he was asleep, waiting, wishing to stay here beside him forever. Seconds later, she slipped out from beneath the sheets. She dressed quickly, silently. It had been like this the last time—Reid sleeping, she sneaking out into the weak night, sad but not ashamed, never ashamed of making love to this man. He shifted in his sleep. She knew she had to hurry and go. Yet, as she'd done that night five years ago, she knelt by the side of his bed and watched him sleep, telling herself to go and unable not to wish it was otherwise.

Still on her knees, she leaned over, let his breath warm her lips one last time. Her body felt deliciously scrubbed as if she could still feel his hands everywhere. She felt full, pretty, powerful, strong. He had given her that.

She looked at the man sleeping. She loved him, had always loved him. And because she loved him, there was only one thing she could give to him.

The truth.

She stood and left without once looking back.

REID WOKE ALONE. The sun was not so high in the sky for people who kept normal hours, but it was late for a man who had always risen before dawn. He gathered the sheets in his fist and brought them to his face. They smelled of the woman.

Danielle.

Last night, he had looked down and she was there. Dani. Danielle. He had heard himself call out the name as if a prayer.

Danielle.

He looked to the clear light filling the room and waited for understanding to come.

There was the morning and the memory of last night and a feeling of completeness and caring. And the only understanding was what had happened last night happened only once, or to a lucky man like himself, twice in a lifetime.

He slid his legs over the side of the bed and sat up, seeing the sun beyond the window and the relief of the land. Perhaps, he wasn't supposed to understand it; perhaps, he never would. All he knew was he'd only experienced this feeling once before, and he'd let that woman get away. He wasn't going to lose this one.

He grabbed a pair of jeans, heard Maria with Trey in the parlor, called out ''Good morning,'' but didn't stop as he passed. Barefoot, he ran across the wet, thick bluegrass and, not seeing Dani or Solstice on the distant track, hurried to the barn. He knew now it had been madness making him go out, meet other women, relying on the past as an excuse to avoid a relationship in the present. He had used every means possible to avoid his attraction to Dani. Still it hadn't been enough. Fortunately, he'd come to his senses before it was too late.

Bennie, pushing a wheelbarrow down the barn's center aisle, stopped and looked at Reid, barefoot, barechested, breathing hard. "What's wrong? Good God, it's not your mother?" He set down the wheelbarrow.

Reid shook his head, moving past Bennie toward the other end of the barn and Solstice's stall. The black colt was grabbing some hay from the net. He stared at Reid, calmly chewing.

Reid turned to Bennie. "Where is she?"

"Uh-oh, what'd Dani do now?"

Reid had to smile. "Nothing. Where is she?"

"She worked the colt early, then drove the truck into town to run some errands."

She hadn't left him.

"She should be back any minute." The older man studied Reid. So did the colt. "Want me to send her up to the house?"

Reid stroked Solstice's ears, saw the sun high in the stall window. "Have her call first, in case I've left for the hospital."

"Will do."

Reid went to the house to shower, dress, see Trey, look over the morning workout times. It was getting late. He had hoped to see Dani before he left for the hospital, but he couldn't wait. He was getting ready to leave when Maria brought in the day's mail. He took the bundle and decided to go through it quickly in case there was something for Georgia. If Dani wasn't back by the time he'd sorted through it, he'd head to the hospital.

As soon as Dani got back from town, Bennie told her Reid had bolted into the barn like a loose horse and wanted her to call the house as soon as she got back. She called the business line first but the machine answered. The private line was busy. She knew he wanted to talk about last night. He would tell her it was a mistake for an employee and employer to become involved, and she would convincingly agree. She put away the new supplies while she waited a few minutes to call the house again. She thought about her visit to the legal aid office this morning. She was going to tell Reid the truth after Solstice ran his first stakes race next week. She could no longer deny him their child. She only prayed he wouldn't deny her the same right. Just in case, she needed to know her legal rights.

She was going to the office to call again when she saw him in the barn's entrance, his shoulders filling the door's opening. She stopped, facing him. It wasn't until he moved toward her, coming in out of the sunlight into the barn's shadows that she saw the anger on his face. He stalked toward her, the dim barn painting him even darker. Her first thought was he was upset she'd left in the middle of the night. She looked at him, saw the sharp silver lights in his eyes and knew it was something more. Fear filled her as the man she loved came toward her.

Not yet. It was too soon. She wasn't ready, would never be ready.

He reached her but said nothing. His head only gestured toward the barn's back door. She understood, but couldn't move, still waiting for the moment not to be happening, something, anything to make it right. He stalked past her. He didn't look back to see if she followed.

Dizziness rose in her from the sight of his proud stiff back, his controlled steps. They walked out into the sunlight. It was a beautiful day, a beautiful, beautiful day, the thought shattering Dani.

Reid stopped a short distance from the barn. It was the pause before he turned around that made Dani realize his anger was becoming uncontrollable. She breathed in, waiting for what was to come. Finally he turned. There was that look again that pierced her flesh. He leaned toward her, challenging her to step back. She stayed, waiting, his hot gaze on her, until she didn't know what was worse, the silence or the words that were to come.

He stepped even closer. Her senses, heightened by fear, received him—the scent of skin, the touch of breath. His fingertip touched her, traced the beat of blood at the base of her throat, drew a line to her chin and tipped her face to him.

"It's been five years, Danielle. Don't you think it's time we kiss and tell?"

Chapter Thirteen

The bright sun behind Reid blurred lines. Forms once solid were vague. She saw only the silver steel of his eyes. Eyes that asked for answers. The silence had ended.

"You remember," she said.

He reached into his pocket, pulled out an envelope and handed it to her. She looked at it. It was addressed to Danielle DeVries Tate. She looked at him.

His gaze held hers, wouldn't allow either of them release. "Not an easy night to forget."

She turned away from those silver rounds, the quiet disdain.

"You wore a green dress."

No, for once, she didn't want to remember.

"And your hair..." His hand hovered above her crown. "It was piled high, curled, red."

Burnt sienna, she silently supplied. Color had claimed her face also. Light and shadow, an accent here, a deepening there. Until in the end, a woman needing no more than a tip of the head or a slow, sidelong glance to reveal her reason for being.

She took a full breath. That was how it had begun.

"Who are you?" The voice cut to the bone.

Only to come to this. She looked up, meeting Reid's silver stare. She saw her son's eyes, felt the panic move across her skin.

She breathed in, trying to bring the distant cool shade inside her where all was fear. She had to tell him everything. She didn't know what he would say or do. His rights were many. She clasped her hands together, the envelope twisting, her fingers twined so that the knuckles popped. She might have been praying.

"It was you, wasn't it?"

She nodded, not yet ready to speak, her eyes wide and pleading.

"What were you doing here that night?"

Her words came quiet and desperate "It was my eighteenth birthday. My father had wanted something special for me. He'd bought me a dress, took me to a salon, hired a car, made all the arrangements. It was only for one night." One night. It had seemed so harmless.

"I didn't expect to meet you." She looked away. "Never did I expect to meet you."

"But you did." His voice was low and even, emphasizing his anger.

She looked at him. "Yes. I did."

He waited for her to continue.

"You smiled at me and asked me to dance, and I

wanted to dance with you more than anything else I'd ever known before. I wanted your arms around me, your breath warm on my skin, the feel of your body against mine, and later…'' Her voice was even softer. ''I wanted it all that night. Everything. Except the truth that the woman you held in your arms would be shoveling out stalls at dawn.''

She lowered her head, lowered her voice. ''I didn't want the truth that night.'' She raised her head. ''Neither did you.''

He stared silently at her.

''So I pretended to be something else, someone else. It was only for one night. One night.''

It had become a refrain.

He looked at her, his eyes hard. ''So what are you pretending now?''

His tone was almost conversational. He'd had five years to perfect his control. She stared into his cold eyes, looking for the man she knew. If she surrendered now, she would lose everything. She had to make him understand, but how? How did one explain the unexplainable?

Her hands raised, appealing ''This is who I am.''

''Is that why you ran?''

''We both knew it was never to be more than one night. One night. We never expected…''

She wouldn't talk of the passion, the pleasure that had come, taken them both. To talk of it now would turn it around. Something special would become only shame. That night had given her Reid, had given her a son, and the only thing she regretted was having given them both up.

Her breath came out trembling. "You came up to me. You took my hand. I never knew…" She fumbled for a rationale where there was none. "I was so young."

"We were all young then."

She knew he thought of his brother. Now her betrayal would be added to the memory of that night.

"What happened that night—" Her voice faltered before the anger aligning his features. She had to tell him. He deserved that much. "What happened that night—" She looked away, feeling awkward and self-conscious as the images of their lovemaking came to her. "Nothing like that had ever happened to me before. No one else could have made me feel like that. No one but you." It was all she could give him now. It wasn't enough

He stepped back, his gaze taking all of her in. "It must have been fate." The words were meant to be hurtful.

"Don't destroy it." She was begging now.

He stepped closer to her, his mask suddenly dropping to an expression so devastated, she felt herself shatter.

"You were the one who ran away."

"I had no choice."

"You had a choice that night."

She wanted to crawl inside him and make him understand. She looked into those wounded silver eyes. "There was no choice that night."

The words hung between them. They both knew she was right.

"Don't destroy it," she whispered.

"Who are you?" he demanded once more.

She untwisted the envelope, smoothed its front. "Danielle DeVries Tate," she recited. She looked up from the white rectangle. "DeVries is my mother's maiden name. She was from South Carolina, youngest daughter of tobacco heirs. Her family disowned her when she married my father. She had hoped giving her child the family name might help them accept her marriage, accept me. They thought she did it out of spite. They've never asked to see me."

"Is that why you lied? Because of the way the wealthy had treated you and your father?"

"They thought my father was only after my mother's money. They were wrong."

"And you were wrong about me, my family. My mother grew up in tack rooms smaller than horses' stalls."

Dani's hand made a sweeping gesture toward the big house, the buildings, the pastures, the hills beyond. "That night…this…this is what I saw."

Her hand clenched, pressed to her breast. "And you saw a woman dressed in emerald silk, painted and poised with the promise of old money and bloodlines. That was the woman you wanted that night. That is the woman I wanted to be that night."

He stared at her. "And what woman did I want last night?"

She looked away. He caught her chin, turned her face to him.

"I took that silk dress off you that night. I took down your hair, kissed away the false colors of your face." His other hand reached for her. His gaze wouldn't let her go. "I saw you that night. You."

"Look at me." She raised her hands, pleading. "Look at me. What do you see?"

He looked at her and desire rose within him. And he despised himself.

"Why did you come here? You had your enchanted evening. Why did you come back to Hamilton Hills?"

She turned her head, the face he couldn't stop looking at now in shadow.

He remembered her astride the colt the morning she had defied him and ridden Solstice. He saw her head tipped to the late morning sun, her eyes half-closed with happiness and pleasure. And himself praying, *God, let it be her. Let it be her.*

He looked at the woman before him now. It seemed his prayers had been answered.

Even now, he tasted her.

His hands wrapped around her arms and he dragged her to him, the space separating their bodies dissolving. The envelope dropped into the dirt. "Why did you come back? Why did you come back to Hamilton Hills? What do you want from me?"

She stared up at him. There would be no waiting until after the stakes race. She looked away, took a full breath. She looked back, meeting Reid's silver stare. She saw her son's eyes. Her son who had slept in her arms. Her son who she had vowed never to leave again.

She saw the man before her. Her son's father.

"I'm Trey's mother."

She saw the shock take Reid's face, sink in, settle deeper on those sharp bones as if he were aging before her. He pushed her away, stumbled back. He stood still, silent, the shock rippling in. His eyes closed, then opened, slowly blinked as if hoping she were only illusion. The sun had shifted. Her words hung in the cool air surrounding them now.

His lips moved. "My brother's son, my brother's son." Shock had turned to disbelief.

The emotion of the last five years rose and threatened to topple her. She squared her feet, thought of her son. Reid's son.

"Your brother isn't Trey's father. You are."

He heard the words and, for a second, there was nothing, no thought, no movement. This was how it'd begun five years ago. No preparation, no warning, nothing but a truth completely unexpected.

A truth that had become a lie.

His senses realigned. He felt the cool air and an even cooler understanding why this woman had come back to Hamilton Hills. "If you're here for the family fortune, you're too late."

She shook her head. Anguish that almost seemed real crumpled her features. "No, no money. I only wanted to be near my son."

His hands clenched her arms again, his fury unchained and terrifying. "He's not your son."

"He is. He is." She was sobbing now, pleading. "He's my son. And your son. He's our son."

He released her, afraid of his anger, her agony. She twisted away from him. He stared at her shuddering back, heard the sound of her sobs. He remembered her words and was without reason. He wanted to go to her, take her in his arms, no longer speaking truths or lies but silently wait for sweetness. He wanted to turn and run until she was only memory once more. He didn't move. She sobbed. To each of her quivering breaths, he silently added his own until all emotion seemed to have left him and he could go on.

"I want you out of here." He turned toward the house.

"I won't give my son up again." Behind him came her cry.

He turned back to her. So small with her blotchy, tear-stained face, she might have been lost. Yet he saw the resolution in her eyes.

"Five years later, you've had a sudden surge of maternal instinct?"

"I didn't know where he was. I didn't know he was with you, your family. My father handled everything. Then I saw you in Saratoga, you and a four-year-old boy. I saw the birthmark on his thigh. My baby had the same marking." She looked away, out to the savannah's forgiving shoulders. "My father told me the rest." She looked back at Reid. "Tests can prove it all."

His mother's genetic sample had already confirmed Trey was a Hamilton but they'd been told it was his brother's son. Reid looked away from Dani's tear-stained face. *Trey was his son?* The world shifted around him. He took a long, deep breath, trying to hold on.

"Why were we told Trey was my brother's son?"

"My father wanted to make sure my identity was protected. He was afraid if you knew the child's real roots, you wouldn't accept him." Her voice dropped. "I was afraid also. That's why I never contacted you when I found out I was pregnant. I was wrong." She looked at him with the face of a woman-child. He looked for his son in those features as if her story might be true.

"Then when I saw you, saw my son running across the Saratoga shedrow, oh, Reid, you can't know." She turned her head as the tears came again. "You can't know."

But he could. He knew what it was like to long for something so desperately, certain you would never find it. And then to have it. He tensed his muscles, closed his eyes to the image of the woman before him.

"I didn't know what to do. All I knew was I had found my son. He had a family and was loved and well taken care of and I had no right, no rights at all. But I couldn't just walk away. I couldn't give him up again. Not then. Not now."

She gulped a breath. "I decided to get a job at Keeneland just to be near him, get a glimpse of him now and again, see him grow. Then, you bought Solstice..." Her hands lifted helplessly. "I can't give my son up again."

Her reddened eyes gazed at him, appealed for understanding. "He's my child. I gave him up once. I won't give him up again."

Reid stared at this woman, this woman he had dreamed of for five years. After she'd disappeared, after his brother's death, he'd never thought he could feel that empty again. He'd been wrong. "If what you say is true—" He held up his hand, halting her avowals. "And I will know soon enough, trust me."

"It is true."

"If what you say is true..." He ignored her assertion. "Exactly what do you expect—visitation rights, shared holidays, joint custody?"

Despite the mockery in his tone, he saw the hope flash in her eyes.

"No." His voice cut the cool air.

The light in her eyes darkened. "I'm his mother."

"And, according to you, I'm Trey's father." It was the first time he'd said the words and again they stunned him. Suddenly, desperately, he wanted them to be true. But if they were...he looked at the woman before him, saw her sitting at the table, he on one side, Trey on the other and the sun on their backs. He remembered her tenderness with the child, her tenderness with him. What was real? What was false?

He breathed deeply, hanging on. "What is it you want?"

"I don't want to lose him again. If the only way I can accomplish that is through the courts..." Her hands lifted, appealing. "What choice are you giving me? What choice do I have?"

"You said it yourself—'there is no choice.'"

"I love him, Reid," she said quietly.

He looked at her, seeing her again with Trey, playing, laughing. He saw the boy in her arms, fast asleep. He remembered her face whenever she'd looked at the child. "I know." He would not deny her that.

Tears were in her eyes once more. "Thank you. And thank you for loving him, too—you and Georgia. I gave him up because I thought it was the best thing for him." She smiled sadly. "It was. But let me be part of his life, too."

He rubbed his brow. He couldn't think clearly—not with her voice softly pleading and the sorrow in her eyes. He glanced at his watch, tried to look detached. "I have to get to the hospital. Obviously this isn't a matter that can be resolved in a few minutes. I need to think, to figure this out."

"Do you think we can figure this out?" Her voice was so hopeful.

He stared at her. Such happiness she had given him. He had been a fool. Yet now wasn't the time to think of himself. He had to think of the child and what was best. "I don't know," he said wearily, turning to go.

"Reid?"

He looked back. She stood small and so alone against the landscape that he loved. "I wish things…" Her hands clung to each other. "I…that night…last night." Her mouth trembled. "I wish everything had turned out like the dream it was."

He stared at her a long second, then turned and

walked away, ignoring his heart whispering the same wish.

SHE WENT BACK into the barn, although she knew there would be no solace there. There would be no solace anywhere. Solstice had been turned out with the others. She was coming out of the barn to empty a water pail when she heard Reid calling her name. She looked to see him coming toward her, and for a second, her heart surged at the sight of him. Just as quickly, she dismissed the feelings and gathered her strength.

"The hospital called."

Please dear God, not Georgia.

"They have a Mick Tate. He's been hurt."

She dropped the bucket.

"They found your name and the number here in his wallet. You should get there immediately. C'mon, I was just about to leave. I'll take you."

She hurried to the car with Reid. They didn't say a word to each other until the car pulled into the emergency room parking lot. "Thank you." Dani opened the car door while the vehicle was still rolling to a stop.

"Wait. I'll come with you," Reid said.

Even though she knew it was his basic decency that made the offer, she was touched. She shook her head. "No, I'll be fine. You go see your mother." She jumped out of the car and ran to the emergency room.

They were wheeling her father up to surgery when

she arrived. She got into the elevator with the stretcher and took her father's hand.

"Dad, I'm here."

He turned and looked at her. "Dani girl," he said, his smile distorted by the swells along the one side of his face. "Guess I didn't run fast enough or far enough this time. Might be time to put me out to the pasture."

She held on to his hand. "You'll be fine, Dad. They'll put you back together good as new, and you'll be prettier than Derby Day."

"A-w-w, Dani." His hand tightened on hers. "I wish I'd done more for you. I did what I could this time. But I don't know if it's enough."

The elevator doors opened. "S-h-h-h," she quieted his rambling. "Don't you worry about nothing." The stretcher stopped before the operating area. She leaned over, carefully kissed her father's bruised cheek. "I'll be right here waiting for you to tell me all about the day you rubbed a Derby winner."

THE OPERATION went without complications and, after an hour in recovery, Dani was allowed to see him. His eyes were closed, his breathing even, but as she pulled a chair up to his bedside, he looked at her and smiled.

She sat down, placed her hand on his. "Came through in the money, Dad."

"Had to," he whispered. He ran his tongue across his lips.

"Here, how 'bout a sip of water." She poured some from the small plastic pitcher into a cup and held it to his mouth. He took a small sip, eased back into the pillows, closed his eyes.

She looked at him bandaged and stitched and bruised and shook her head. He opened his eyes. "They did a good job this time, didn't they?"

She looked away, not wanting him to see the worry on her face. "Oh, I don't know." Her expression under control, she looked back at her father. "You're still here, aren't you?"

He smiled. "That I am." His expression sobered. "But, just in case the bastards do the job right next time, I've got a story I've been saving for you."

She heard the slur in his voice. "S-h-h-h. You should be resting now. Why don't you get some sleep? I'll be right here, and we can talk when you wake up."

"No. You need to know this in case something happens to me."

"You're going to be fine, Dad."

"Listen to me, Dani girl. You know I was against you going to Hamilton Hills, but I see you these past few weeks happier than I could ever do for you. Now, I never gave you much, hell, I gave you nothing—" He paused to swallow, raised his hand as her protests began. "But I'm going to give you something now to make sure no one takes away that happiness."

She shook her head. "Dad, listen—"

"No, you listen before whatever's dripping into my veins here knocks me out for the night. I wasn't the only one who didn't want to see you at Hamilton Hills. That fat-assed attorney always puffing on those foreign cigars as if he were Castro himself was none too pleased either. The bastard has been on my butt since you showed up there.''

''Otto? Otto Powers?''

''That's right. Ot-to.'' Mick dissected the name into two distinct, disdainful sounds. ''I told him let my girl be. She don't know anything.'' Mick shook his head. ''No, that wasn't enough. There you were, so happy, not hurting anybody and still every day, he was calling, threatening until finally, he says, if I couldn't get you off Hamilton Hills, he would.''

Mick rolled his eyes, the only movement that probably didn't cause him pain. ''That's when I had to do a little threatening of my own and tell the son of a bitch what would happen if he bothered me or you again. I told him.'' Mick looked down the length of his battered body. ''Now, twenty-four hours later, here I am.'' He winked, wincing from the pull of the stitches. ''With room service and everything.''

''You think Otto Powers had this done to you?''

''Now, that I can't swear by. Might be a mere coincidence. I do have some slightly overdue debts, and you know how cranky those collectors can get. On the other hand, Otto wasn't exactly cordial when I told him yesterday if he even breathed your name to Reid Hamilton, I'd take him all the way down with me.''

A sick feeling started in the pit of Dani's stomach. ''Otto handled the adoption for the Hamiltons, didn't he?''

''And for me,'' Mick said.

Dani didn't understand. ''Isn't that like a conflict of interest or something?''

Mick smiled dryly. "That was the least of the counselor's worries at that time."

Dani's sense of dread grew. "What else was Otto Powers worried about?"

"The findings of the investigation."

"The insurance investigation?"

Mick nodded. "Following the deaths of the horse and the oldest son."

That night. That night. "What happened that night, Mick?"

Her father rubbed his chin, flinched when he hit a tender spot. He looked into the far corner of the room. "Beautiful creature, that Aztec Treasure. Pure poetry. They say he wasn't that bad when he began, a bit of a honey even, but then came the fame and the crowds, and then they oversold his breeding rights. He earned his keep, all right, but the market was becoming glutted with his foals, the Treasure was getting older and more unbearable, being forced to breed more while his price was going down. And the Hamilton farm was going with him. Of course, nobody knew all that until afterward. Nobody knew it that night except the older boy running the place and Otto Powers."

Mick tried to reach for the water cup. Dani held it to his lips, waited for him to take a drink.

"I was up in the loft that night. I was watching for my girl. Saw you too, darling." Mick smiled his crazy-looking crooked smile. "I was a good distance away, mind you, but I spotted you. A young man was leading you out to the dance floor and Lord, even from far away, you looked like a dream."

It had been a dream, she thought. A dream that had become a nightmare.

"What happened in the barn that night?"

"I heard someone come in the back door, so I hid behind the bales. It was the oldest Hamilton boy—the one who ran the farm. I watched him go into the stallion's stall, a fistful of hay in his hand. I heard someone come in after him. The boy heard it too, and turned to the back door. It was then I saw the small hammer in his hand. Ball peen, they call it. Slender, almost delicate tool. Not big enough to do a heavy job—no, just a small task—say crack a cannon bone no thicker than my finger. One small tap—that's all that would be needed to take a horse down forever."

Dani swallowed, felt sick.

"It was the lawyer who came in through the back. I didn't know who he was at the time—later I made it my business to know. The two men started arguing. The boy was saying he didn't want to do it, but he had no choice. *Go ahead, then,* the old man told him. *Go ahead and do it.* The lawyer stood there, waiting. The stallion was prancing and pawing by this time, mind you. Never a calm one to begin with, you could see he'd sensed the men's fear. Hell, I was holding my breath myself. Such a magnificent creature. The boy bent down, picked up the animal's foreleg. I wanted to close my eyes, but I couldn't. It was like when you've got to crane your neck when you pass a car wreck."

Mick released a breath. "Then the boy, bless him, bowed his head and began to cry. Sobbed just like a baby. The hammer fell right out of his hand. The lawyer went over, helped him up. The horse was completely confused by now. I heard a vehicle pulling up outside. The other men heard it, too. The boy pulled himself together, the lawyer picked up the hammer, ushered them both out of the stall, dropping the hammer in the grain bin just as the security guard came in. 'Everything's just fine in here,' the Hamilton boy told him. 'I was just showing Otto here the Hamilton pride and glory. Why don't you go on up to the house and get some of those prime-time refreshments?' Then they left—all three of them.''

"But how did—"

Mick looked at his daughter. "How did Trey Hamilton and that magnificent creature end up like they did? Well, after they all left, I went down and dug the hammer out of the bin.''

"Why?"

"The rotten part of me was thinking, 'You never know when something like that might be useful,' and the virtuous part of me—'' Again Mick tried to wink but only winced. "—was thinking, 'No, that beautiful animal deserves better than that.' What if that Hamilton boy changed his mind and came back? Treasure was riled up righteous by now between the men and the fighting and the music and noise coming from yonder. He was kicking his door something fierce, and I noticed the door's bottom bracket hadn't been hooked. I was about to go latch it when I heard someone coming again. As I went out the back door, I saw the Hamilton boy again, hoped to hell he'd come back only to bolt the door. Heard him trying to calm the horse down, saying, 'Don't worry, boy. No one's going to hurt you—not me, not anybody.' That's when I left.''

Her father looked at her. ''With the hammer that had the Hamilton boy's prints on it and the lawyer's.''

''And Otto knows you have it,'' Dani added. ''That's why he arranged the adoption and didn't ask any questions.''

Mick leaned back into the pillows, but his manner wasn't triumphant. ''Like I said, you never know when a little thing like that might come in useful. Now I want you to know where it is—in case, anything happens to me.''

She shook her head.

''We'll call it your inheritance. If Otto ever threatens you, just wave that little tool under his nose, and he'll let you be. You won't ever again have to worry about anyone making you leave your son.''

Chapter Fourteen

Reid sat in the clear cold, the morning cracking open all around him. The reds, oranges, golds that had painted his land passionate would soon be gone. Winter would come and the world would quiet.

He looked down at the plastic bag he held in his hand, at the slender hammer inside the clear cover. *No more silence,* she'd said.

He'd sat dumbfounded when she'd given it to him. He sat dumbfounded still. He'd asked her, "How many secrets do you have?"

She'd shaken her head, that lovely-shaped crown taught by the Thoroughbreds to express so much with a turn, a toss. "No more. There're no more secrets."

"And I'm to believe you? Believe this story?"

Her green eyes were dull. "That will be your decision."

"You do realize your father could be charged with blackmail? Withholding evidence? Obstruction of justice?"

Her eyes were without fear, without any emotion at

all. "If you promise not to file any charges against my father, I will leave you and our son alone. I will not file for visitation or custody rights in return for my father going free."

He had looked down at the hammer. "You could've gone to Otto. Once he knew you had the hammer, you probably could have gotten anything you wanted."

"I only wanted my son."

"Otto could've arranged visitation, partial custody, whatever was necessary to protect him. Instead you've given it all up—" He saw the first and only sign of emotion in her eyes. "For what reason? To protect your father? That could've been more easily accomplished by your silence."

Her head had reared up. "No more silence."

He'd stared at her, still not understanding why she would raise suspicions about her father, why she would give up that which mattered most. It was mutiny without any bounty. "Why?" he'd finally asked once more.

"Because you needed to know," she'd said, rising from the chair opposite him. "You needed to know the truth."

She'd left him then. He'd sat for the rest of the numbing night, the thin weight of the hammer lying in his lap.

DAWN HAD NOT quite ended, and all the many windows were still dark in Otto's house. Otto opened the door after the fifth ring of the bell, muttering, "For the love of Mike,'' as he gathered his untied robe around his waist.

His face turned ashen when he saw Reid. "Not Georgia."

Reid shook his head, stepping past him into the tasteful foyer. He turned and faced his family's oldest friend

Otto studied him "What is it, son?"

Reid pulled the hammer from his jacket pocket. Otto's expression wore the shock of surprise for less than a second. His professionally-culled facade followed too quickly and convicted him

Reid's hand holding the bagged hammer shook. "All this time you knew."

Otto sat down on a rosewood chair that looked too delicate for his girth. "And what do you know?"

"Dani Tate is Trey's mother."

Otto's voice was trained. "I was professionally obligated to protect her identity."

Reid looked down at the hammer. "And personally obligated."

Otto stared at the tool. "What else do you know?"

"Everything."

Otto closed his eyes, his smooth expression falling. He opened them, a weary old man. He looked at the hammer, its steel head, rounded on one end, flat on the other.

"In the end, he couldn't do it, you know. Your brother, he couldn't do it, he couldn't hurt anything he loved. He loved you and Georgia, too. That's what took him into the barn that night. That and his pride.

He was so damn proud." Otto looked at Reid, nodded toward an upholstered bench. "Sit down, son."

Reid stayed standing.

"I took the hammer from him. We left the barn. I thought it was over—the worst of it." Otto sighed. "It was only the beginning."

He looked at Reid. "You were young when your father died, but Trey was the oldest son, almost a man. Your father had left the responsibility of the farm, the family to him. He felt he'd let you all down. He said he'd do anything to save the stables. In the end, he did."

"Why'd he go back to the barn?"

"He didn't think the door had been latched properly. He was afraid if Treasure got to kicking and..." Otto's voice trailed off, came back stronger. "I wasn't going to let his death be in vain. It was an accident—your brother's death, the horse's injury. There was no reason not to collect on the insurance."

"So you hid the truth?"

"The truth? What is the truth? You tell me, because I don't know." He eyed the bag. "I thought I knew. Then I got a call from Mick Tate, learned he had the hammer—the hammer with your brother's prints on it, with my prints on it. And the truth became a matter of who was telling the story."

Reid stared at the slender tool.

"If that hammer had been turned over, you and your mother would've lost everything," Otto said.

"And you would've also," Reid pointed out in a strangely rational tone.

"No." Otto's voice became fierce and unrepentant. "I wasn't going back. Neither was your mother." His face twisted as if poverty and shame were a stench that had slipped in beneath the massive twin oak doors and permeated the elegant foyer.

"You sent the letter." It wasn't a question. "Did you have the old man beaten up, too?"

"Harmon Fox offers you a partnership not only with his farm but with his family, and you're sitting in the kitchen, holding hands with a stable worker. Was I supposed to sit back and watch you blow an opportunity like that? For what? A tumble in the hay with—"

"Don't." Reid held up his hand, his voice steel, an astounding violence within him. "Don't."

Otto folded his arms, his complacent expression saying *I rest my case.*

"Dani's gone." He heard his voice, the words, and for a beat, disbelief. "Leave the old man alone. Do you hear me?"

Otto looked up at Reid. "Your brother was dead. That couldn't be changed. What good would it have done if the truth were told?"

Reid dropped the hammer onto a cherry table. "I would have known," he said quietly. "I would have known."

It RAINED for three days and three nights gently like a woman weeping. There was no racing on the turf. The mudders became favorites.

On the second day, Georgia came home from the

hospital. On the third day, she asked where Dani was. Reid hesitated, worried it was too soon after her illness and surgery to know the truth. Then he heard Dani's voice—*No more silence.*

So he took his mother's hands in his and, starting with that night five years ago and ending with his dawn visit to Otto, he told her everything. When he finished, Georgia sat silently, looking a long way off. Reid looked down at their joined hands and wondered if he'd been wrong to tell her.

"You know they say there's no such thing as a black Thoroughbred?" She finally spoke. Reid looked up at her, his worry increasing.

"No such thing as a white Thoroughbred either. We think we see it. We'll even say the animal is black or white, but if we look closely, we see their coats are actually a blend of light and dark. It's an illusion. Black, white. They don't exist."

Reid stared at her, confused, worried.

"Now the whole time I'm listening to this story, I'm looking for the black and the white, but I can't see them. Then I remembered. They don't exist."

Her silver eyes looked at her son. "So many people doing what they think is right and yet, everyone seeming so terribly wrong. Who's right? Who's wrong? Anyone? Everyone? I don't know. I don't know. There's no black or white."

She shook her head, the smile that had always sustained Reid softer, wistful. "I've had a husband, sons." She laid her hand against Reid's cheek. "I have a grandson, good friends, a good life. Yes, there's been great sadness but also great joy. And in the end, what I'll remember is the love, so much love."

She squeezed her son's hand. "So I listened to this story and I looked for the black and white, but how can I find them? They don't exist. And so, in the end, all I find is love."

"Love?" Reid drew back, then stood, went to the window, seeking his land. "Love?" he spit out again. He turned and looked at his mother.

Her pale, lovely face was a calm oasis. "Your brother's love for his family first took him to the barn that night. His love for the animal brought him back. A father's love for a daughter also brought him to the barn that night...and brought her to you."

Reid turned back to the window.

"Otto's love for this family made him hide the truth. And there's Trey...who has brought so much love to this house as if made for nothing else."

Reid took several steps to the next window.

"And it was Dani's love for you that gave you the truth you needed so desperately to know."

Reid closed his eyes, shook his head. He turned to his mother, his voice angry. "So, forgive and forget— that's what you're saying?"

Georgia smiled gently. "At least, forgive."

Reid shook his head again as he sank down in the chair opposite her. "I don't know, Mama. I don't know."

She caught his hand in hers. Her silver eyes looked into his. "Yes, you do, darling. Yes, you do."

THE RAIN ENDED, leaving Keeneland washed and clean and reflecting its own light. Dani walked to the barns in the early, coolest hours, her thoughts going no further than each step she took. What was before ceased to exist and what was to come not yet born. Only now was here, and the days passed in a series of images, detached and easily forgotten as a senseless dream.

She had gotten a job grooming at the racecourse. She'd said goodbye to Solstice, standing before him without words. Words had never been necessary. She'd put her palm to his glossy neck. He'd looked at her, then stepped to the side and lay down. He'd picked his head up and looked at her again until she'd sat down beside him, resting on the broad expanse of his side. They'd stayed like that for a long time, stretched out in the heat of the straw, Solstice picking up his head every now and then to gaze at her.

She hadn't said goodbye to Trey though. As promised, she hadn't gone near the child again. She had waited, seen him outside with the collie and Maria and had watched until they went back in the house. Then she'd left Hamilton Hills, her thoughts going no further than each breath.

At Keeneland, she'd worked tirelessly, grateful for the continuous cycles of feeding, bathing, walking, wrapping, rubbing, filling her days with endless labor and her nights with physical exhaustion.

Yet, despite her ceaseless campaign, there were moments when she would remember. Silent seconds when she would think of the child who still was hers in her heart. She would see the land's soft splay, the brows of the hills and remember Georgia, the gentle matriarch of it all. She would see Solstice who had earned her looks of rue and wonder and never doubted he deserved them.

And she would think of Reid, how he had taken down her hair, slipped his arms around her from behind to the skin beneath her shirt and laid his cheek against the slope of her back.

Once the sadness had come in such a crippling wind, she'd wrapped her arms around her thinness and been forced to her knees. Doubled over in pain, she'd softly sobbed as another groom's wife had come and placed one hand on her shoulder and murmured *Cara mia.*

The first feeding of oats was finished, and it was time to parade the horses in front of the trainer. Dani went to the chestnut filly, said to have a sophisticated timing that made her seem a natural champion. She would be running in the big stakes race today. So was Solstice, Dani thought, and then thought no further.

Reid had arrived at four-thirty that morning. He stood beside Smiley in the stands now, watching the morning workouts. Solstice had been running like a freight train, but there was a recklessness, a wildness to his motion. He also pawed, squealed, snapped his teeth and butted his stall until Bennie threw up his hands and swore at him in Spanish. Other times, he'd stand still as stone, his ears pricked forward, listening to the sounds that came to him on the breeze.

One sleepless night, Reid had gone to his stall. The

horse had been lying down but was awake. He lifted his head, passed his tongue over his lips and blew out a breath. Reid stared back. The animal had sighed once more, but levered himself up and stood, snorting once at Reid before dropping his head and pressing his nose to the man's chest.

"I know," Reid had said, stroking the colt's neck. "Just the sound of her voice had been enough."

DANI LED the filly to the paddock, measuring her steps to the hoofbeats beside her. The course faced west to the full sun, and she dipped her head against the light, looked to her charge, the filly's coat the brilliant browns and reds of the season. She concentrated on the animal's graceful neck arching, the flare of the filly's nostrils as she sniffed the air, the stone cold legs, white ankles, silvery heels. Still Dani thought, Reid was here somewhere in this same light. Her gaze moved back to the filly's pretty head and she saw a kind eye.

BENNIE WAS LEADING Solstice, Smiley was murmuring to the jockey and Reid was to the rear, following them. They hadn't reached the paddock yet when he saw her. For a second, there was nothing, no thought, no movement. He'd known she was at Keeneland. Still he stood silent, his eyes closing, then opening in a slow blink. She was still there.

She was standing with her back to him but he'd recognized her instantly as if he'd been looking for her. He had, he realized. She turned to give the jockey a leg up, patted the chestnut's neck, and handed the animal off. She watched the animal head to the track. He couldn't look away. Certainly his memories had been false. She stood, surrounded by the colors of silks and the fullness of harvest, more beautiful than his mind had imagined.

This was how it'd begun, he thought, going back to that night five years ago. This is how it would always be between them—a vision, a half-dream, fire.

Smiley touched his arm. The trainer's gaze had followed Reid's, seen her also. He looked at Reid but said nothing, only nodded toward the enclosure where the others were waiting. Reid nodded, looked back once more. Dani was gone.

SHE BLENDED into the crowd facing the sun, never looking at anyone directly. He was here with Solstice, possibly Trey, too. The thought made her misstep and she almost stumbled until a stranger's hand came out and righted her. "Thank you," she mumbled, moving on into the deepest, thickest part of the crowd.

As soon as she looked to the oval, she saw Solstice, gleaming and glossy, his head impatiently bobbing, and she smiled against the tears that threatened. The horses were led into the gate, there was the clang of the bell, then the streaks of brown and black and roan broken only by the shimmer of the jockeys' silks. There was the muffled sound of hooves and the building response of the crowd and from the back of the field, Solstice and the chestnut filly pushing each other, moving up into the main group. Into the clubhouse turn, the horses were just behind the two leaders, dueling stride for stride. As they spun into the stretch, only a length behind the leaders, Solstice made the move that stopped hearts as he pulled wide. Dani was smiling now. The colt left the chestnut behind, drove past the number two, then the number one horse, the black and gold colors spread across his back and horse and rider shining in the autumn Bluegrass sun. As soon as he crossed the finish line, a length in front, Dani closed her eyes, heard the roar of the crowd and, for one second, felt no pain.

GEORGIA AND TREY were sitting beside Reid in their box as Solstice won. Reid had watched that midnight colt barrel down the stretch and knew this was only the first of many important victories for this dark beast…and for Reid. He smiled, certain Dani had seen Solstice's run also and was somewhere not far, smiling too.

Georgia patted his hand resting on his thigh. His fingers entwined with hers as he lifted her hand and kissed it, then pressed it to his cheek in gratitude.

"Did we win?" Trey asked.

Reid looked down into the silver eyes that matched his own. Silver eyes that only had to blink, and everything made sense. He pulled the child who had always been his son onto his lap. "Solstice won."

He stood, lifting the boy in his arms and placing him on his shoulders. "Now it's our turn." He looked down at his mother and winked. "We'll meet you in a few minutes?"

She winked back. "I'll be waiting."

DANI WAS LEADING the filly beneath the stands when she heard Trey call her name. She knew this time she didn't imagine it. She'd stopped imagining a week ago. She froze. The other groom in the outfit walking with her threw her a curious glance, but agreed to take the filly back to the barns. Still Dani didn't look behind her until she heard her child call her name once more.

Reid saw her turn, her fingertips touching her cheek, confusion and longing on her face. He lifted Trey off his shoulders and set him on the ground. The boy looked up at him and he nodded. He watched as Trey ran toward Dani. The emotion on her face was overwhelming.

She smiled and squatted down as their child came charging toward her. "Trey." Aware of Reid's gaze on her, she offered the boy her hand hesitantly.

Trey grabbed her hand and, catching her unaware, pulled her into his embrace, wrapping his arms around her shoulders. Reid saw Dani inhale deeply into the curve of the child's neck, but her arms remained rigid on the boy's narrow back. She lifted her head, her gaze such a painful mixture of question and pleading that Reid started toward her as he nodded and murmured, "It's okay, it's okay."

She needed no more than his first encouragement to gather the boy into her embrace. She lifted him, her arms holding him to her, her hands cradling his head as she closed her eyes and rested her forehead on the child's crown.

Reid reached them and Dani's head jerked up. Trey leaned back to look at her. Reid stood so close, the boy's head rested against his chest. "Where've you been?" their child asked.

Dani looked down at him, smiled bravely. "Right here." she said

"Here?" Trey was indignant. "Come home now. I missed you."

She blinked hard several times. She shifted Trey to her right hip, turned her head away so he couldn't see her face. Still Trey's hand reached over, touched her cheek. "It's okay. Daddy 'plained everything. You're my mommy."

She looked at Reid, emotions moving so swiftly across her face, he couldn't define them. He laid his hand on hers. His heart jumped. Fire. Fire and fear.

"It's okay," he said, reduced to the eloquence of a four-year-old.

So much uncertainty and pain in those light green eyes. He touched the curve of her cheek. He felt the warm press of her flesh. The flare of hope inside him. God help him. He was a goner.

"Come home," he whispered. "Come home."

She stared at him, her eyes bright with questions and unshed tears.

"I've loved you since that first night...that first sight." He bent and touched his lips to hers.

"Yuck," Trey declared. Dani's lips moved against Reid's with a sound of sweet, uncertain laughter. He smiled down into the bright green of her eyes, took her face gently in his hands. Not to be outdone, Trey slung a soft arm around her neck.

This is how it should be, Reid thought, this woman, their child, arms all around each other, holding on tight. He never wanted to let go.

"Marry me," he said.

His arm tightened to steady her. He felt the fine trembling in her body.

"Yeah, marry 'im, Mommy," Trey urged.

She looked to her son's devilish grin, then back at Reid, her smile shaky, her eyes wondrous as they searched his face. "I thought..." Her voice quivered. She squeezed her eyes tight, but still the tears slipped past and slid down her cheeks. She buried her face into Reid's neck, not wanting Trey to see her tears. Reid glanced at the boy. The child patted his mother's back and nodded with the wisdom of the ancients as he whispered to his father, "Women."

Dani lifted her head, laughing through her tears. "I love you," she told Trey, kissing his cheek until he giggled.

She turned to Reid, her expression becoming solemn, her eyes glowing with joy. "I love you."

Reid smiled. "Is that a yes?"

"Oh God, yes. Yes," she said as he kissed her brow, her cheek, her mouth.

"C'mon," he said, his arm staying tight around her as he ushered them back toward the stands. Dani saw Georgia waiting for them, smiling and nodding approval as they came toward her. She saw Smiley, Bennie. In the center, she saw Solstice who stared right through her but pricked his ears and rolled an eye when she patted his neck and said, ''Good job, fella.''

Together they stepped into the winner's circle, Reid's arm strong around her, Dani holding fast to him, to Trey's small body sweet between them. Bound by the bonds that wouldn't let go—blood, flesh, love, above all, love, they turned to the camera and smiled into the Bluegrass sun.

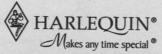

If you enjoyed what you just read,
then we've got an offer you can't resist!

Take 2 bestselling love stories FREE!

Plus get a FREE surprise gift!

HARLEQUIN®

makes any time special—online...

eHARLEQUIN.com

your romantic books

♥ **Shop online!** Visit Shop eHarlequin and discover a wide selection of new releases and classic favorites at great discounted prices.

♥ **Read** our daily and weekly Internet exclusive serials, and participate in our interactive novel in the reading room.

♥ **Ever dreamed of being a writer?** Enter your chapter for a chance to become a featured author in our Writing Round Robin novel.

your romantic life

♥ **Check out** our feature articles on dating, flirting and other important romance topics and get your daily love dose with tips on how to keep the romance alive every day.

your community

♥ **Have a Heart-to-Heart** with other members about the latest books and meet your favorite authors.

♥ **Discuss** your romantic dilemma in the Tales from the Heart message board.

your romantic escapes

♥ **Learn** what the stars have in store for you with our daily Passionscopes and weekly Erotiscopes.

♥ **Get** the latest scoop on your favorite royals in Royal Romance.

All this and more available at
www.eHarlequin.com
on Women.com Networks

HINTA1R